A Shadow's Kiss

KIRSTEN S. BLACKETER

Dedication

I would like to thank fellow authors Em Taylor, Whitley Gray, and Beth Trissel who shared their advice and expertise when my own research proved inadequate. My critique group and beta readers for sacrificing their time to read the story and make it better. You know who you are. And my editor, who kicked my butt to make this story shine. I thank you all!

As always, my husband, who in the midst of his duty to his country, still finds time to make me and the kids the center of his universe.
I love you, babe.

Table of Contents

Chapter One

Scotland, Summer 1329

The warm summer breeze wrapped around Madeline as she caught a glimpse of the tall, fortified keep. It was her family's home. *But not mine.* A twinge of regret pierced her heart.

"You are thinking of him again, are you not, Kitten?" Angus asked, bringing his horse up alongside hers. The youngest of her brothers, Angus had always been the most intuitive. They had a close bond, one that sometimes made it hard to keep any secrets.

Madeline felt the rush of warmth flood her cheeks. *Am I that obvious?* "What makes you say such a thing?"

She nudged her horse forward, ignoring her brother's intense gaze. Over the past few days, her mind strayed to the people she left behind. Evelyn, her uncle, the servants she had befriended, and, of course, Sir Alexander. The hillside surrounding the keep was littered with tents and banners. She wondered why there were so many people, when her brother's response broke her musings.

Angus caught up with her. "You get this far away look in your eyes when he crosses your mind." He chuckled. "You have worn a forlorn expression for most of the journey."

She huffed. *No use fighting with him.* He knew her better than most, even after a prolonged absence. Truth be told, her mind fluttered with concern about the family she had left behind. When Angus arrived during the tournament, it had caught her off guard. Then he whisked her away in the midst of the commotion. She still had no idea what happened, if anyone had been hurt or, worse yet, if anyone had died. Fear clawed at her insides. Angus had done his best to reassure her, but she worried about her cousin, Evelyn. She had caught a glimpse of Evelyn before they disappeared in the crowd, but was she well? Days later, and Madeline remained in torment over questions plaguing her.

The two of them rode through the main gate. Ten years had passed, but still the castle intimidated her with its size. As they entered the inner bailey, she saw her father standing tall, wearing a plaid of earthen tones, a graying beard covering his jaw. His eyes were sharp and bright, narrowed against the sunlight. Her heart leapt. Then she noticed the line of tall, handsome men beside him. Her remaining four brothers. At the end stood a girl of around ten, her hair a wild mess of tangles. Madeline's heart caught in her throat. *Could it really be?* She dismounted and strode toward her family. *The squalling infant who heralded the end of their mother's life.* Pushing the intrusive emotions away, she approached her father.

"Father," she said with a smile. He scooped her into a hug, her feet dangling off the ground. When he released her, his eyes were moist.

"Och, lass. I never thought I would see you again," he said, a slight crack of wavering emotion in his voice. "You are the spitting image of your mother. God rest her soul." His gaze lingered on her a moment longer, then he cleared his throat and turned to the men beside him. "You remember your brothers?"

She greeted them, tipping her head in a polite nod, the way she had been trained. They had changed so drastically in appearance; it would take her time to warm up to them again. They wore plaids matching their father's and each had a broadsword fastened across their backs. All of them were striking men. They watched her with curious eyes.

"And your sister, Heather." Her father pointed to the wild-haired girl on the end. Madeline approached her, kneeling down to meet the girl's inquisitive eyes.

"Heather, 'tis a pleasure to meet you," she said, offering the wee lass a smile. The girl arched her brow and glanced at her father. When she returned her eyes to Madeline, she proffered a halfhearted curtsey.

"My lady," the girl replied through gritted teeth.

"You must call me Sister," she said, clasping Heather's hand in her own. "For that is what we are." The girl's face lit up at the contact.

"Welcome home, Madeline," Angus said. A chorus of whoops and hollers joined in as her brothers surrounded her. This is what she remembered. The informality and the boisterous commotion of her highland family. While she had been raised a lady, Madeline felt the highland air seeping into her, bringing her back to her roots.

"Enough," Rodric, her eldest brother, yelled above the others. "Let us get our sister settled now. Leave her be." Madeline grinned at him when he offered her a wink of understanding. "Angus, show her to her chambers. The rest of you, get your sorry arses back to work."

A soft tug on her hand reclaimed her attention. "Can I come with you?" Heather asked her eyes luminous.

"Aye, little sister. You can come with me." She squeezed her hand gently.

"Och, you are holding up the festivities," Angus grumbled from the doorway.

Madeline's head snapped up. "What festivities?"

Angus glanced around, a guilty expression plastered on his face. She turned to her father. "What is he talking about, Father?"

He appeared no less guilty. "I should have had Angus tell you, but I asked him not to do so." He took a deep breath. "We are hosting a tournament." A sudden dread filled the pit of her stomach. "The winner will receive your hand in marriage."

"I am to be a prize!" Madeline's outrage echoed off the walls of the bailey. Bad enough she would be forced into a marriage not of her choosing. She had convinced herself she would go through with the arranged union for duty and honor. But the idea of being a mere prize to be won unleashed a fury inside her. Perhaps her cousin, Evelyn, had influenced her after all.

"Father," she began, her voice calm as her mask of *delicate lady* slid into place. "I wish this had been brought to my attention before I arrived." She glared at Angus, who had the good sense to blush and duck inside the great hall.

"Aye, you deserved to know what you were walking into," he said, his deep voice softer. "I wanted to give you a better chance." He sighed. "Go settle in, we can talk later." He hugged her again. "'Tis good to see your smiling face." Her father left her standing there, her jaw hanging askew.

"Would you like to see your room now?" Heather's insistent voice drew her attention.

"Aye," she said, burying her father's news deep inside. "Would you lead the way?" Madeline would be strong, despite her agitation at the unwelcome surprise.

The girl's lips split into a toothy grin. Madeline returned the infectious smile. The initial apprehension at meeting Heather melted into a deep love at the girl's expression. She saw trust and admiration in her sister's eyes. Madeline stood determined to strengthen their bond, her heart swelling with love. *Her sister.* Together they disappeared into the great hall.

The situation, which had called her home, had been less than ideal. She shook her head. *For better or worse.* She joined her brother who waited near the hearth, irritated they intended to use her as a pawn. *Politics.* She had known she would be required to marry at some point, but, deep down, part of her wanted to be able to make the decision for herself. No point in pining for what could never be. Her duty lay with her family.

Madeline straightened, gripping her sister's hand tighter. If only she had been able to tell Sir Alexander, then maybe things would have been different.

Angus tugged on a stray curl hanging from her braid. "Glad to be back home? Mind you do not go wandering the keep late at night."

She turned to him, wagging a finger in his face. "Do not dare even think about playing any pranks on me, Angus Campbell. I know where you sleep."

"I would not dream of it, Kitten." His charming smile held no mischief, merely humor. "But I would hate to have one of our esteemed guests back you in a darkened corner."

Madeline swallowed the lump of fear threatening to choke her. She would prefer the pranks to such a fate. "All the same, I have learned a few things from Evelyn to protect me from them and you." His smile, the only response he gave, spoke of a challenge accepted.

Alexander left the keep five days ago. Had he come to his brother's aid faster, Gabriel's injury could have been prevented. He hung his head, steeling himself against the mountain wind, hiding his shame. He had failed both his brother and the one woman who mattered to him. As soon as word reached him Gabriel's fever had broken, he had saddled his horse and set off to find Madeline. Evelyn had kept her promise to do everything in her power to save Gabriel. He would be eternally indebted to her.

The unnaturally dark skies loomed overhead as Alexander rode into the Scottish highlands. Perhaps it was an omen, though he never held much belief in superstitions. His heart clenched at the knowledge of Madeline being here, presumably against her will. He had to find her, discover what had happened. Nudging his horse into a canter, he continued through the brush.

Images of harm befalling her in a hundred agonizing ways tormented him. He could not push his horse any harder than he already had. Fear clenched in his chest. *What if it is already too late?* He thrust the thought aside and focused on the path before him.

When Alexander crossed the border, he had changed into a dark plaid, pulling the black hood of his cloak down to shield his face. Anonymity would keep him safer as he traversed Scotland. While his loyalty remained to the English Baron of Rayne, he would always be part Scot and a Shadow Guardian. This combination made the road he traveled much more dangerous.

That fact might be the only thing to help him find Madeline. He had been a fool, confessing his feelings to her in the garden less than a fortnight ago. Wearing his brother's garb always made him more impulsive. He had seen her in the moonlight, her face turned up to the stars. Alexander pulled her into his arms and kissed her, savoring the sweet taste of her lips and the heat of her pressed against him. He never would have dared to take such liberties with her had he not been dressed as the Shadow Guardian. He swore, when he kissed her again, she would know exactly who was kissing her. He grunted, shoving the memory aside. It made his chest tighten with a longing he could not explain.

As he cleared the hill, he glimpsed a small village overshadowed by an intimidating, well-fortified keep. *This must be it.* Urging his horse forward, he made his way down the hillside. The last inn had told him Campbell Keep lie a day's journey north. Banners and tents surrounded the keep, littering the hillside. Alexander estimated at least five hundred in the encampment. As he approached the village, he felt their gaze on his every movement. Their stares and whispers did not bother him, but they did prepare him. He stopped at the tavern, dismounted, and handed the reins to a young boy standing outside.

"Watch him for me?" he asked the lad, who appeared no more than ten. He slipped the boy a coin. "There is another in it for you if you take good care of him." Alexander's voice slipped into a Scottish brogue. He took no chances. Not when there were still those who hated the English with a passion.

"Aye." The boy's eyes lit up as he tucked the coin into his pocket. Alexander smiled and slid the hood back. He stepped into the tavern. The loud ruckus of voices mixed with rowdy laughter echoed off the walls. A handful of serving women wove expertly through the throngs of drunken men. He found an empty table tucked in the back. Their curious gazes followed him as he passed. Alexander tried to blend in with the crowd.

"What can I get for you, love?" a buxom serving maid asked. Her smile and appreciative gaze hinted at her willingness to serve him in all ways.

"Ale and a hearty stew if you have it." She nodded and licked her lips as she walked away, throwing a little sway into her hips.

Alexander never allowed himself to be distracted by a

woman. *Except Madeline.* She haunted him, since the first moment she had entered his life. He trained harder, trying to find his edge again. But she had dulled it with her sweet disposition and lithe figure. Every time her hazel eyes sparkled and her golden hair caught the sunlight as she turned to watch him pass, an arrow of desire lodged itself in his heart. Shaking his head, he forced himself to focus. His duty: find and return her to the baron's safekeeping. Exasperated, he ran his hand over his face.

"You look like you could use a drink," a gruff voice said. "Here." The stranger sat a mug of ale in front of him.

"My thanks." Alexander glanced up.

"Mind if I join you?" The stranger plopped into the chair across from him not waiting for a reply. "You here for the games?"

"Games?"

"Aye." The man took a drink of his ale and turned his sharp green eyes on Alexander. He chuckled. "You are not from around here, are you?"

"Nay."

"A man of few words. Not the worst trait you could have."

He stared at the stranger. "Do you require something from me?"

"Your name would be a good start."

"Alexander," he said, drinking deeply. "Who are you?"

"Angus. Are you hungry?"

"Aye." He motioned to the barmaid. "I have a stew coming."

"Och, to hell with the slop they serve here." Angus stood. "Come. Join me in my father's house. He is feasting tonight, in honor of my sister's return."

Alexander's head snapped up. "And is this a momentous occasion?" he asked, letting his instincts take over.

"Aye, she has been gone these last ten years, fostered with relatives in the south." Angus grinned. "But now she has returned home. Come." He downed the last of his ale.

Alexander wondered what kind of cruel trick fate was playing on him. "Does your sister have a name?"

"Madeline," Angus replied, turning toward the exit.

Alexander nodded. It seemed as though she had gone of her own volition. His original plan had been to slip into the keep unnoticed, collect Madeline, and then leave before the alarm could be raised. He followed Angus from the tavern. Although the details of her disappearance had been brought to light, his mission remained the same: locate Madeline. It would be up to her, remain or return. He tossed an extra coin to the lad holding his horse and grabbed the reins, following the gregarious Scot toward the keep.

What waited for him inside those walls, he could not hazard a guess. He prayed Madeline would not betray his secret. An English knight had no place behind Scottish stone.

Chapter Two

The great hall was decorated with festive banners and a grand feast had been prepared. Madeline sat at the head table with her father and brothers. Her gaze lost in the contents of her trencher. She mixed the contents of her trencher with the tip of her knife, her appetite vanished along with her hope of happiness. A hundred pairs of eyes watched her every move. Unused to being the focus of such attention, she wanted to crawl under the table with the dogs.

Six neighboring clans had arrived at her father's summons for the tournament. Each clan presented a son to compete for her hand. Madeline felt their gazes as she sat there and nibbled at her food, the smile playing on her lips never quite reaching her eyes. She promised her father she would do her duty, but that did not mean she had to like it. Her most sincere hope would be the winner would be anyone except the Douglas heir.

His cold gray eyes roamed over her with an intensity that made her want to curl up under a blanket and hide. They held a dangerous hint of mischief Madeline had seen before in a hawk assessing its prey. She took a sip of her wine and avoided meeting anyone's gaze. The door to the great hall swung open, and she heard her brother, Angus, shout his greetings. *'Tis about time he showed his face.*

"Father," he said. "I would like to introduce Alexander. He hails from the south."

Madeline choked on the sip of wine she had just taken as her head snapped up. She swallowed as delicately as she could, forcing herself to remain calm. Her hand trembled. *It could not be.* The stranger's broad shoulders stretched as he tipped his hood back revealing thick mahogany hair and ice blue eyes. Her hand flew to her throat. *Why is he here?* Her heart leapt. *Has he come for me?* She forced the delight into submission and sat patiently waiting for him to glance in her direction.

"My laird." He proffered a slight bow. When he rose, his gaze fell on Madeline. She sat forward, her mouth poised to speak when she saw him shake his head. He returned his attention to her father. "I thank you for your hospitality."

Madeline's jaw snapped closed. She leaned back in her chair. *What is he playing at?* His voice sounded deeper with a rolling Scottish lilt. *Sir Alexander.* Those broad shoulders and profile gave him away, and she could never mistake his eyes. Ever. Madeline had spent far too many nights dreaming about him to forget even the slightest detail.

"Where are you from, Alexander? Who are your people?" Her father's questions were curious and polite. She watched the exchange between the men, her mind spinning with questions.

"My mother is a daughter of Clan Kerr, from the south, near the border," he said.

The sound of the Scottish brogue on his tongue brought made her breath quicken and her body warm. *It suited him.* She licked her lips absently as his gaze flickered over her.

"What brings you this far north?" the laird asked, leaning forward.

"I am searching for answers," he said. She heard the hesitancy in his voice. Had she not known him, she would have missed it. Alexander was not lying, but his words were not completely honest either. He was a terrible liar. She strived not to smirk, remembering several occasions when his half-truths had been directed at her. Tonight, she would have the truth from him, if it killed her.

Her father did not pry any further. "I hope you find what you are after."

"I have," Alexander replied, his gaze settling on Madeline for a brief moment before returning to the laird.

Her father nodded and held up his cup. "I pray you, sit. Join our feast. You are welcome in my home and at my table."

Alexander bowed, and with a passing glance in her direction, he joined Angus at the far side of the head table. She sat there, her stomach in knots of apprehension, waiting and watching. *I must speak with him, but how?* Madeline nibbled on some bread. The sound of laughter brought her attention back to her brothers. *Alexander, laughing!* She stared at him in complete disbelief. *Who is he truly?* The Alexander she knew never laughed, and he certainly could not be Scottish. Her eyes narrowed. He caught her scowl and tipped his cup to her, a grin on his lips.

With an agitated huff, Madeline begged her father's pardon and left the great hall. The memory of Alexander's good humor haunted her as she approached the staircase leading to her chambers. Somehow she had to speak to him. She knew of one way to catch him alone: discover where he slept.

As Madeline disappeared around the corner, Angus chuckled. He noticed Madeline's interest in Alexander from the moment he showed his face. During the remainder of the meal, she had cast sidelong glances at their new guest, her eyes bright with curiosity. He tapped his finger on the side of his cup.

"Alexander, would you consider joining the festivities?" Angus asked on a whim. There had to be more going on beneath the brooding exterior Alexander presented. It had ensnared Madeline, and now he meant to fetch out every detail, since it was his duty as an older brother to protect his little sister.

Alexander's easy smile disappeared. "What purpose do they serve?" He bit into a haunch of mutton.

"To win Madeline's hand in marriage," Angus said, a smirk playing on his lips. He took a drink of ale and nodded, waiting for a reaction.

"And why would I want to do that?" Alexander met his bold stare, his eyes glinting like ice in the winter.

"Are you daft? Did you not see the way she stared at you?" He arched his brow. Of all the men in the room, Angus could not imagine one of them catching his sister's attention. He had been right. She had barely even glanced at any of the suitors when her father introduced them. But this southerner caught her attention before he even spoke. If he had known any better, he would have thought she already knew Alexander. No mistaking the way she devoured him with a single glance.

"Nay, I had not noticed." He indulged in another drink. "I should be on my way. I thank you for the meal." Alexander stood. Angus grabbed his tartan and pulled him back down into his seat. The stunned expression on Alexander's face nearly made him laugh.

"You are stayin' here." Angus crossed his arms. "There is no lodging to be found within leagues of the keep. Come. You must be tired from traveling for so long. Take my chambers for the night." He stood and motioned for Alexander to follow him. Together they slipped into the dark recesses of the keep, ascending a staircase winding up into a corridor housing the main chambers. "Here." Angus pushed the door open. "If you need anything, just shout."

"My thanks," Alexander said as he beheld the chamber. "I shall be leaving on the morrow."

"Think on my suggestion," Angus said, a grin tugging on his lips. "The tournament shall begin the day after the morrow. I will take my leave." After he left Alexander, he walked past his sister's chambers. The door had been left open a crack. He hesitated, indecisive. Raising his hand, he knocked on her door. She appeared quickly, pulling it open. When she saw Angus, her face fell.

"Aye, what do you want?" Her eyes narrowed.

"Can I not make sure my own sister is well?" he said in a cheerful tone. "I saw you leave the feast early and wondered if you were ill."

"Nay, I am well enough." She glanced down the hall. "Has your new friend left then?" He caught the flash of curiosity in her eyes before she shuttered it with indifference.

"Alexander will stay the night in my chambers, but he claims to be leaving on the morrow," Angus said, leaning against the doorframe. "I invited him to join the tournament, but he declined." Angus shrugged as if it made no matter to him whether Alexander stayed or left.

"Why would you—" she started, but caught herself. "Why

would he want to marry a highland lass? Och, makes no difference to me. All those men are alike. They do not really want me. They want a *prize*."

He reached out and tipped her chin up, forcing her to meet his gaze. "Kitten, any man would be proud to have you for a bride. Do not sell yourself so cheaply." He wanted to say more, wanted to reassure her it would all work out in the end. Angus pulled her into his arms, kissing her forehead gently. "Get some rest. You have a long journey ahead of you." He winked then left her to her thoughts.

There was something there. Try as she might, Madeline could not hide the desire for the southern stranger in her eyes. It betrayed her. As he walked out into the summer night, he remembered he had seen the longing in her eyes before. When she spoke of the man she left behind.

Alexander sat on the bed and rubbed his hand over his face. Things could not have gotten more complicated. Admittedly, he had been relieved to see Madeline hale and hearty. She looked fresh and wild. Seeing her unbound hair nearly made him forget himself. It required all his strength not to stare at her, not to seek her out in the great hall.

The door to his chambers opened. As if summoned by his thoughts, Madeline slipped inside the room. Her forest green gown highlighted her hazel eyes as she turned to face him.

"Madeline." He breathed her name. It whispered across his lips like both a prayer and a curse. "What are you doing here?" He stood to confront her.

"I might ask you the same question, Alexander." She shelved her hands on her hips, her gaze angry and defiant. The spark of life in her eyes brought a smile to his lips. "See, what is that? A smile? Over the past several months, I have never seen you smile. Who are you? What are you doing here?"

His grin vanished as quickly as it appeared. "You

disappeared without a trace, Madeline. The baron sent me to determine your safety and return you to his care."

"My uncle sent you." Her words were thick with disappointment. "That is the only reason you came, because of your sense of duty."

"Aye," Alexander said, speaking a half truth. He would never admit the real reason to anyone. He had petitioned the baron to send him, to let him cross the border and risk his own safety to find her.

"So this—" she waved her hand at his garb "—is all an act."

"Aye," he said. "'Tis complicated, Madeline."

"It always is," she replied with an exasperated sigh. "So explain it to me." She crossed the room and sat down in a chair by the hearth.

He blinked, surprised by the tenacity so unlike the little mouse he had known at Keep Rayne. The fire in her eyes burned as brightly as the one flickering in the hearth. He knew she would not leave until she had her answers.

Alexander sat on the edge of the bed. "My mother is the only daughter of the Laird of Clan Kerr. That is no lie. My father had been a lord and a knight, a knight in the service of King Edward." He sighed. "The marriage had been complicated by the loyalties of each family. In the end, my mother joined my father at his English estate."

Madeline's lips were parted as she leaned forward. Her loose braid trailed over her shoulder and disappeared into the top of her gown. He swallowed and continued his tale.

"I was fourteen when my father died. My brothers and I were already squires for a neighboring lord. My brother, James, inherited the title, while Gabriel and I decided to continue in our quest for knighthood. My mother and sisters returned to her ancestral home in Scotland. They live there still." Alexander took a breath and met her gaze. He noted the way her lip was drawn between her teeth as she listened to his story.

"So you are from both worlds. Why did you choose your father's heritage over your mother's?" she asked. He heard nothing but curiosity in her soft tone.

"At first I chose my father's path, hoping knighthood would gain me a place in the world." He shook his head. "But it only brought pain. So, I petitioned the king for a place of service with the Baron of Rayne, a man known for his honor and his pledge for peace between the two nations. It became my mission to serve the realm by maintaining peace on the border, thus satisfying the loyalty to both halves of my heritage."

"So you are using your Scottish heritage as a cover. To be sure, many of the clans still do not trust the English. Their wounds have not yet healed. And we are not known for our forgiving nature." She offered him a weak smile.

"Aye." He hung his head. "I shall leave on the morrow and inform the baron of your safe return to your family. Lady Evelyn will be pleased to hear this news."

Madeline's expression brightened. "She has returned safely?" Alexander nodded. "Oh, thank heavens." A flush covered her cheeks. "I cannot believe in all the commotion I forgot to inquire after my dearest cousin. Am I such a horrid creature, to forget Evelyn?" She buried her face in her hands.

Alexander crossed to where she sat and knelt before her. Taking her hands, he caressed her palms with his thumbs and met her gaze. "She is home, safe and happy. I assure you." Her eyes filled with tears. "You have been ripped away from one family and restored to another. Two halves of yourself need to mend. You did not forget her, and I fear you never shall." He smiled, trying to cheer her.

"There it is again." She stared at him in awe as he brushed the tears from her cheeks.

"What?" He glanced over his shoulder, then back at her. "Where is what?"

"Your smile," she said, a grin tugging at her own lips. She removed her hand from his and smoothed her fingertips along his beard roughened jaw.

Alexander beat down the urge to kiss her. Her touch set fire to the already smoldering embers he kept burning for her. "Madeline." He sighed. "I..." His voice trailed off as her hand slid into his hair, tangling with the fine strands at the nape of his neck.

"In the time I have known you," she whispered, leaning closer, "You never once smiled, never looked at me, barely even spoke to me." Her lips hovered inches from his. He could see the gold flecks amidst the swirls of blue and green in her eyes.

"Aye," he murmured, afraid to trust his voice.

"But you risk your safety to see to my own. Out of duty?" Her fingers tightened in his hair. His hand slid up encasing her wrist, his thumb pressing against the tender flesh where her pulse beat like a drum.

"Aye." The lie slipped from his tongue so easily, and it burned him to the core to speak the word. Her destiny lay in marriage to another, better for her to never know the delicious agony she wrought within him. His heart lodged in his throat, threatening to choke him if he uttered another word. He should stop the madness, pull away from her. But she tempted him like a siren's song, luring him closer with every breath.

Her gaze dropped to his lips, and she leaned back, her hands slipping away from his touch. A rush of painful relief washed over him. He nearly gave into his selfish desires, nearly confessed himself for the fool he truly was.

He recognized the pain etched into every sweet curve of her face. His rejection injured her as if he had raised his hand against her. Smoothing her dress, she stood. He followed suit, waiting for her to say something, anything. But as quickly as he recognized the pain, it disappeared from her face as the sweet façade of a lady slipped into its place. A twinge of guilt and regret stabbed him in the chest. He wished he could take it back, but they both had responsibilities and nothing could change that.

"Will you deliver a letter for me?" she asked, her voice wavering beneath the forced strength.

"I shall do whatever my lady commands," he replied. Her tear-dampened gaze fixed on his. He regretted the words the moment he spoke them, but they were the truth and all he had to offer her.

"I shall go write it then. May I give it to you in the morning?"

Little minx, she knew exactly what she was doing. He would not be able to slip out at dawn as he had planned. He would be forced to bid her farewell, forced to see her one last time in the morning light with the highland breeze in her hair, her eyes moist with unshed tears. Curse her for knowing him so well. "Aye. I shall wait for you by the front gate at dawn."

She nodded, gracing him with a smile, which did not touch her eyes. He led her to the door. Turning, she pressed a hand to his chest. His heart ceased to function.

"May God grant you mercy, Sir Alexander," she said as she rose on her tiptoes and pressed a chaste kiss to his unshaven cheek. Without another word, she disappeared down the hall. Alexander closed the door with a shove and rhythmically beat his head against the stone wall. The sooner he returned to the baron, the sooner he could forget the Scottish lass who had stolen his heart.

Chapter Three

Alexander stood in the bailey, cinching his saddle, when Angus approached him.

"Leaving so soon?" he called out, a lopsided grin on his face. Alexander nearly rolled his eyes. Would he be harangued by every member of the house before he took his leave? He had hoped to slip from the keep unnoticed, but he still waited on Madeline and her promised letter.

"Aye," he replied, turning to straighten his tack and saddlebags. "I was hoping to get an early start."

Angus leaned against the horse's rump watching Alexander. "You should stay for the tournament," he said, taking a bite of the pastry in his hand. "My coin would be on you."

"Is that so?" Alexander cast him a sidelong glance. "You would be bettin' on the wrong man." The brogue was coming easier now since he heard it all around him.

"You should stay then, prove me wrong." A devilish gleam sparkled in Angus' eyes. Alexander pressed his lips together, afraid he may say something he would not be able to take back. "Listen," Angus said, stepping closer. "You are a man who likes to keep to himself, I ken. But you are passin' up an opportunity few ever dream of."

Alexander turned to him with a sigh.

"I do not know you from the next man. But I have never been wrong when it comes to my gut." Angus tapped his stomach with his fist. "You are not like these other knavish apes, panting after my sister like a dog in heat. You have an air about you bespeaking honor and duty. Something the other men lack." He leaned closer. "She deserves a man like you."

"You do not know what you are saying." Alexander dismissed him with a wave. Angus stepped back.

"Look at her and tell me there is naught special about my sister, and I will leave you be." He gestured behind him and walked away.

Madeline was crossing the bailey, heading directly for him. Her braid sparkled like golden threads had been woven into her hair. Loose tendrils framed her face. The deep blue of her gown absorbed the morning light, making it shimmer as she walked. Her eyes remained on him, even as her brother passed, she did not so much as glance at Angus.

"Good day, Alexander," she said, a smile on her lips. Everything about this seemed wrong. He should leave, just get on his damned horse and leave, but he stood there caught in her web. "Here are the pastries I promised," she said, then added in a low voice, "The letter is tucked inside." Handing him the package, she brightened. "I bid you a safe journey, good sir." Her gaze lingered a second longer, and the words stuck in his throat.

"Many thanks, my lady. You are most generous." He damn near choked on the farewell. With a halfhearted smile, she returned to the embrace of the great hall.

Tucking the package into the saddlebag, he leaned his head against the smooth leather surface.

"You are a fool if you walk away." Angus' voice broke his moment of tormented silence.

With a glare, Alexander faced him. "You win, lousy coxcomb." He jabbed a finger into Angus' chest. Her brother was grinning like a fool. "I will compete in your tournament."

Angus clapped a hand on his shoulder. "Come," he said, grabbing the horse's reins. "Let us get you ready."

Alexander followed behind him. *What the hell have I gotten myself into?* He never broke his own rules. He had to return to the baron and his duties on the border. A part of him, deep in the dark corner of his mind, began to laugh. Gabriel had jinxed him. His mother always said, when one fell, the other would follow. If he won Madeline's hand, his mother would finally get her wish.

Shaking his head, he disappeared into the stables with Angus to prepare for his first experience in a highland tournament. A grin split his lips as the image of Madeline's reaction to seeing him on the field filled his mind.

Furious with Alexander, Madeline wandered the field outside the keep. How could he be so cold? Had she misunderstand the heated look he gave her the night before? She swung her arm wide, wanting to hit something, to strike out of anger. For years she played the dutiful lady, minding her tongue, behaving as she had been instructed. There had been many times she wanted to lash out like her cousin, Evelyn. Be strong and independent. But where had it gotten her dear cousin? Kidnapped by a craven madman.

Madeline spotted the archery targets near one of the tents. A line of bows and quill of arrows sat against the tent wall. While Evelyn had trained with her bow, Madeline participated in a lesson or two but only rarely since many disapproved of a lady indulging in such an activity. Her palm itched for the feel of the smooth wood in her hand, to feel the tension coil as she drew the arrow back. With a soft curse, Madeline picked up a bow and a single arrow. She glanced around and saw no one.

The wood slid against her skin, comforting and familiar. Nocking the arrow, she pulled the bow up and slowly drew it back. Her arms trembled at the pull of tension. Aiming at the target, she exhaled and released the arrow. With a solid *thwack*, her arrow sang true, striking just below the center of the target. Her heart raced as she picked up a second arrow. She aimed and sent it to join the first, but it hit too low again. Furrowing her brow, she reached for a third.

"Aim just above where you want to hit when shooting from this distance." A deep, familiar voice rumbled behind her. Madeline spun around, the bow dropping to her side. Alexander stood with his arms crossed, his expression unreadable. "Here," he said, stepping toward her. "Let me show you."

Madeline stepped back as he approached. "I thought you had left," she stammered, her heart fluttering at the sight of him. His broad shoulders filled out the linen shirt, and his body wrapped in layers of plaid. She licked her lips. He appeared more dangerous now than he did when clad in chain mail and a coat of plates.

"Your brother, Angus, made a very convincing argument for why I should stay."

Her mouth hung open. Before she could ask him what Angus said, he put his hands on her shoulders and turned her around. Facing the target, she took a breath to steady her hands.

"What are you doing?" she asked as he stepped up behind her. His heat melted into her back, she wanted to sway into him, lean her weight against his body. But she forced herself to stand straight. He tipped the bow up.

"Nock your arrow," he said, as he guided her fingers to position it. "Aye, like that."

His breath caressed the side of her face as he leaned beside her. His left hand covered hers on the bow, while the light caress of his right hand guided hers as she drew the string back. Her heart raced, thundering as a storm of desire raged inside of her. His scent of leather and horse mingled with the highland air. She forgot to breathe.

"Now aim just above where you want the arrow to strike," he whispered. Her eyes drifted closed. "Release."

She let the arrow fly. It struck the target dead center. He stepped away. A small groan of disappointment left her lips as the moment ended. She turned to face him, not caring about the damned target anymore.

Alexander watched her, his lips curved into a hint of a smile. "With some practice, you could become proficient with a bow."

Madeline put the bow back with the others. "Why are you still here, Alexander?" She sighed. Her heart ached at the sweet torture of him standing so close. She had resigned herself to her fate. She would marry the winner of the tournament out of duty and respect for her family name. Taking a deep breath, she faced him again. "Have you nothing better to do than torture me with your presence?"

"You wish me to leave then?" His eyes betrayed nothing, but his voice held a hint of regret.

"Aye." She turned away from him. Why must he do this to

her? What pleasure did he get from seeing her torn with indecision and sadness? For two months, she prayed he would take notice of her shy glances, her flirtatious smiles. Now she was promised to another, he spoke to her. How cruel could fate be? "Leave."

His hand came to rest on her shoulder. "Och, Madeline," he said softly as he pulled her into his embrace. Her arms encircled him, and she buried her face in the folds of his plaid. He tipped her chin up. Seeing the handsome knight brought the heat flooding to her cheeks.

"You deserve to be happy. Does the thought of a life with any of these men bring you joy?"

Madeline shook her head. "My happiness does not matter. I must do my part. Father requires an alliance to unite the clans."

"Aye," he said, stroking his fingers down the side of her face. "But what do you want?"

"It does not matter," she said, disentangling herself from his embrace and taking a step back. "I shall marry the winner of the tournament." Her heart sank at the expression on his face. She shivered at the sudden chill and wrapped her arms around herself. "I should return to the keep before my father misses me."

Madeline walked back to the bailey, the silent tears cooling her warm cheeks. She disappeared into her chamber before anyone could see her and ask any questions. Sitting next to the window, she leaned her face against the cool stone.

A soft knock echoed in her chamber. Wiping the tears with the back of her hand, she stood. "Enter," she said as she reached for her embroidery.

Alexander stood in the doorway. She stared at him a moment.

"You should not be here," she said approaching him. "You must leave before someone sees you."

"Not before I do this." He pulled her against him. When his lips touched hers, the sensation ignited a dormant need inside her. Her body caught flame like dry rushes, devouring her in a heartbeat. His beard scratched against her cheek as he deepened the kiss. Her arms looped around his neck, fingertips sinking into his hair. His hands cupped her face, holding her as though she were a delicate flower. She sighed against his mouth, blooming for him. He tasted her.

How many days and nights had she dreamed of this? Of being in Alexander's arms, feeling his body against hers, his mouth hot on hers. She had been kissed once before, but it had been a brief, unexpected incident. One moonlit night in the gardens within her uncle's keep, a hooded stranger appeared from the shadows. He had taken her in his arms and kissed her. It had been lovely to be sure, passionate, aye...but this was all those things and more. Alexander surprised her yet again. Could there be more to this man than she had previously assumed?

"Alexander, I would appreciate if you would stop kissing my sister." Angus' words shattered the moment. As quickly as it started, the kiss ended. Alexander stepped away.

"Pardon me, my lady," Alexander said. "I overstepped. Pray forgive me." He disappeared down the corridor, leaving a stunned Madeline with her fingertips pressed to her lips.

Her gaze snapped to her brother, who leaned against the wall. His eyes alight with a familiar mischief. She turned away, too embarrassed to face him.

"Go away, Angus." She closed the door and leaned against it. She swore she heard laughter echoing from the other side.

Chapter Four

Once safely inside his chamber, Alexander ran his hand through his hair. The kiss never should have happened. None of it. He meant only to tell her he decided to stay. He pinched the bridge of his nose. Seeing her holding the bow strung tight and watching as she loosed the arrow, he'd been mesmerized. Something had snapped inside of him. He never expected the prim and proper Lady Madeline to use a weapon with such accuracy. She surprised him yet again. Now he wanted her even more than before.

Alexander should not have followed her back to her room, but he could not ignore her reddened eyes and damp cheeks. Although she tried to hide it, he had noticed. The need to comfort her overwhelmed him, making him powerless to resist the pull of her wounded heart. The kiss tipped him over the edge. Her lips were sweeter than he remembered and her curves more full. He punched the bed in frustration. He should have left that morning, put it all behind him. Now all he could think of was winning her hand, but he could not, not without exposing his true identity. A man born of two worlds could not swear fealty to both.

Alexander glanced up at the sharp knock on his door. "Enter," he said. Angus stepped into the room.

"We must speak," Angus said his tone serious. He closed the gap between them. "When I fetched my sister, she wore a sad smile when she believed no one was looking. One, which bespoke lovesickness. Last evening, her sad smile vanished. It disappeared the moment you showed your face." Angus met his gaze. It burrowed into his soul.

Unflinching, Alexander returned it. "What are you trying to say?" Alexander let his façade drop.

"Och." Angus wore a lopsided grin. "See, I was right. You are not Scottish." He rocked back on his heels. "You must be the one Maddy has been pining after." He nodded, unsurprised by his discovery.

Alexander allowed several moments to let those words sink in. "Let me leave. I shall go without incident. No one would be the wiser."

"That would not be advisable." Angus shook his head. "You have already stolen her heart. God knows how long she has been smitten with you. But you cannot leave yet."

"I should at least inform your father of my true identity," Alexander demanded. "Should he find out from any source but me, it would put everyone in an uncomfortable position."

Angus nodded. "It would be wise to inform him as soon as possible," he agreed. "Shall we go together now then?"

"Aye," Alexander replied.

Together they descended to the great hall where the laird waited with his other children. "Father," Angus began. "Might we have a word with you in private?"

The laird glanced up from a roll of parchment, his brows furrowed. He stood. "Excuse me, boys." Turning to Angus and Alexander, he motioned for them to follow. The trio moved into an adjoining room, which resembled the baron's presence chamber. "Speak quickly, there is still much to be done before the tournament begins."

Angus stepped forward to speak, but Alexander put a hand on his shoulder, stopping him. It fell to him to confess himself and set things right.

"My laird, I have been sent by the Baron of Rayne." Alexander dropped the brogue he had picked up on his mother's knee. The rolling cadence came more and more naturally the longer he stayed north, so setting it aside was not as easy as he had believed it would be.

The laird's brows rose in surprise. "You are English?"

"My loyalty lies with the baron, aye." Alexander straightened, unsure where this conversation was leading.

"So you lied?" The laird crossed his arms, leaning against the massive desk.

"I withheld certain truths," Alexander explained. "Fetch

Madeline if you do not believe me. I have known her since I was taken into service for the baron. She can vouch for me."

"Why did the baron send you?"

"Father," Angus cut in. "I fear the fault lies with me. When you sent me to fetch Madeline home, I arrived in the midst of a tourney. I had every intention of speaking to the baron, but a flurry of chaos ensued. I grabbed Madeline and we ran. I fear it made her disappearance seem suspicious."

The laird studied Alexander. "Is this true?"

"Aye," Alexander continued, "There had been an attempt on the baron's life during the tourney. Because of all the confusion, a day passed before we discovered Madeline had gone missing. The baron and I feared the man behind the assassination attempt had taken Madeline as a hostage or some other terrible fate had befallen her."

"So the baron sent you to be assured of her safety." The laird stroked his grizzled chin. "For this I must give you credit. You ken what would happen if you were discovered for an Englishman? Especially this far north."

"I do," Alexander said, turning to Angus. "It was not my intention to deceive you. I merely meant to confirm her safety and then return south. I had not intended to stay this long."

"You could have left at the break of dawn, with no one the wiser, and yet here you are." The laird was sharp. "Why do I believe there is more to this story than you are telling me?"

"He is in love with Maddy." Angus blurted the words before Alexander could think of a reasonable response. He already had one foot in the loch, might as well dive in.

The laird's gaze narrowed on Alexander. He swallowed hard, not sure if he should run or reach for the sword on his hip.

"Is this true?" the laird asked, stroking a hand across his beard. Alexander took a breath and nodded. If he had any hope of escaping with all his parts intact, it just dove off the tallest parapet. "And how does my daughter feel about your affections for her?"

"She does not know," Alexander replied in all honesty.

"How do you explain the kiss?" Angus chirped with a laugh.

"Och, do not tell me that was the first time." He hung his head, laughter bubbling from his chest, his face blotched red from the humor.

"*Haud yer wheesht!*" the laird snapped, effectively silencing Angus and Alexander. His gaze focused on Alexander again. "You kissed my daughter, under my own roof."

"Aye." Alexander shifted his weight, his hand resting at his side, although he wanted to connect his fist with Angus' jaw. The urge to strike the man overwhelmed him. Madeline's brother stood beside him snickering, his hand covering his mouth. "It was wrong of me to take such liberties, I crave your pardon." He hesitated for a moment before continuing. "I have admired your daughter for a long while, but I realize, too late, we both have duties leading us in different directions."

"You intended to leave then?" The laird took a step forward.

"Aye, as soon as you release me, I shall be on my way." Alexander meant every word. If he had overstepped, then he would bear the consequences and leave post haste. Nothing more he could do. His duty and his brother lay in wait for him in England.

The laird did not speak. He walked to the window, stroking his beard, consumed in thought. Alexander exchanged looks with Angus, who shrugged then broke into silent laughter.

"I cannot believe that was your first kiss," Angus whispered.

"Not my first kiss," Alexander snapped.

"So you have kissed a woman before or you have kissed my sister before this morn?"

"I refuse to indulge your curiosity." Alexander ground his teeth together, knotting his fists in his tartan to keep from throttling Angus in front of the Laird of Campbell clan, who just so happened to be his father. Aye, nothing good would come of acting on this impulse.

"So you have kissed her before?" Angus asked, a smirk playing on his lips.

Alexander turned, willing his face to be a mask of indifference. "Ask her, if you wish to know so desperately." He hated baiting Angus with what he would surely interpret as a challenge, but Alexander could not bring himself to explain anything to the man. Not with the brute grinning at him. He really did want to knock all his teeth from his head.

"Enough, both of you," the laird commanded as he turned around. He approached Alexander and laid a hand on his shoulder. "I appreciate your honesty. 'Tis a mark of a true knight and a good man. Although I wish you had been honest with me from the start, I understand why you could not." He dropped his hand. "I do have a proposition for you, though, if you are willing to do me a service."

"What service can I provide, my laird?" Alexander inclined his head, unsure of what the old man would propose, but he would not deny him the right to ask. He nodded, waiting for the man to explain in more detail.

The laird grinned. "I called this tournament for two reasons. The first is to gather all the clans together with the promise of my daughter's hand to the winner. But my secondary motive is stronger. For the last year, someone has been stealing my cattle and raiding my villages. I need to discover who has been stealing from my lands." His expression turned dangerous and quite serious. "My sons cannot uncover the thieves' identities without suspicion. A man with no past, no loyalties to Clan Campbell, could slip into the encampment easily and uncover information which may prove valuable."

Alexander saw the strategy and sense in the plan. He would have to distance himself from Angus and the other Campbells in order to gain the trust of the other clans.

Laird Campbell continued. "You must participate in the tournament and become a worthy opponent to the other competitors. I have no doubt you can match their wits and their strength. Do what you must to bring them into your confidence and they will spill their secrets to you, lad."

Alexander cleared his throat. "If it pleases you, my laird, I would like to represent my mother's family in the tournament. I did not lie when I said my mother's clan is Kerr."

"Very well, lad. Your mother's family holds power in the

south, near the borderlands. It does not surprise me. You have the look of a Scot." The laird turned back to his desk and gathered a stack of parchment. "Angus, see he is properly equipped to join the encampment."

"Aye, Father." He turned to leave the room. Alexander followed him into the great hall. Once they reached the far side and stepped out into the bailey, Angus faced him. "I shall keep my eye on you," he said as they made their way to the storehouse.

Alexander nodded, unsure if he should be comforted by that statement or concerned for his own well-being.

Chapter Five

Madeline paced her chamber. *How can I have been stupid enough to kiss Alexander?* Her heart thundered in her chest, she willed it to stop. Alexander made it clear he intended to leave, returning to the baron and his life in England. She longed to stop him, to join him, something. *Anything.* It tore at her heart he did not even put up a fight when her brother interrupted them.

She collapsed on the bed, thrashing about, allowing herself a wee tantrum. Madeline wanted to scream at Alexander, at Angus, at her father, at the imbecilic highlanders who believed her to be a prized broodmare. At that moment she realized why Evelyn raged against it all, fought tooth and nail to change her fate. The sudden memories of her cousin allowed the tears to come freely. She missed Evelyn. She wished she had gotten to see her return, to hear her laughter once more. Alexander promised she had been safely returned home, and he would not lie to her. *Would he?*

"Evey, what I would not give to have you here," she whispered to the empty room, emotion bringing her brogue to the surface. "I beg your pardon for judging you so harshly, for not listening to your heart." The tears spilled over her cheeks, dampening the top of her gown. She barely heard the door open.

"Maddy?" a child's voice murmured. *Heather.*

"Come in, lass," she said, wiping the tears away. "Sit with me. What are you doing wandering the keep alone?"

Her little sister beamed up at her. A piece of her heart twisted at having left her behind all those years ago. "I do as I please," Heather said with pride.

"Do you really?" Madeline helped the girl climb up onto the bed next to her.

Heather puffed out her chest. "I am nearly grown," she said. "Nanny does not like me running off on my own. She tries to make me a lady, but I would rather be out riding or shooting with

Angus."

"You know how to use a bow?" Madeline asked, a bit surprised.

"Aye, and he says I shall get better if I practice." Heather paused then glanced up at her sister with wide green eyes, her wild auburn hair framing her face. She resembled a highland pixie. "Do you shoot as well?"

"I do," Madeline confessed with a sly grin. "But I cannot be as good as you are, for I never practiced."

"Father says you are to marry the winner," Heather said, twisting a lock of her hair. "I hope 'tis not the Grahams. Liam Graham is a heartless beast." She leaned forward conspiratorially. "I saw him strike a serving girl."

Madeline swallowed the bile rise in her throat. "Where did you see this?"

"I snuck into the kitchens. Cook always sets tarts aside for me. I heard voices in the buttery, and, when I looked, I saw him and the serving girl fighting. Her clothes were ripped, and she was crying. When she spit at him, he raised his hand like he was going to hit her." Heather said quietly. "I tripped over the flour. He heard me, so I ran before he could catch me."

"Did you tell anyone of this?" Madeline asked.

"Nay." Heather shook her head vehemently. "He stares at me, like he knows I was there. I saw him."

"Hush, my love." Madeline opened her arms, inviting her sister into her embrace. She held her tight and rocked her. "Do not fret, there are a half dozen men competing in the tournament. He will not win my hand." After a few moments, she tipped the girl's chin up. "Now," she said in her most sisterly voice, "Let us do something with your hair."

"Och, Maddy," Heather whined. "There is naught wrong with my hair."

"You must be presentable," Madeline replied. "You look like a wild stallion that got caught in the briars. Go fetch my brush off the ledge there."

Heather climbed down, snatching the brush. With a sullen pout, she climbed back onto the bed and turned her back to her sister. Madeline untangled and smoothed her sister's hair. Heather asked her questions about the baron and her cousin, Evelyn. A knock came at the door.

"Enter," she called as she plaited the last few strands of Heather's hair. "There," she said, "That was not so bad, was it?"

Heather turned as the door opened. "Angus," the girl squealed as their brother entered the room.

"Wee hellion!" he said, dropping to his knee. He scooped her into his arms, spinning her around. "Your hair is glorious. Leave it to Madeline to tame the mess we have tried to wrangle for years. I was about to cut it all off." Kissing her head, he set her down. "Run along, I must speak with Madeline. I heard cook calling for you, smells like she has been baking sweets again."

"Would you like me to bring you some?" Heather asked as she turned to Madeline.

"Save it for me, I shall be down in a few moments," she replied with a grin. Heather bounded from the room, her eyes bright with the promise of sweets and her sister's company.

Angus closed the door behind her, and Madeline rose from the bed. She had forgotten her anger toward at Angus but seeing him revived it. Crossing her arms, she faced him.

"What do you want? Have you not caused enough trouble already?"

"Are you still sore at me for ruining your first kiss?" Angus asked. She nearly raised a hand to him, just to smack the half-hearted smirk from his face. He was mocking her. The heat rose into her cheeks.

"'Tis none of your concern, brother." She returned the hairbrush to the ledge.

"Was that the first time he kissed you?" Angus' voice rang in the small room. "Sir Alexander. Has he kissed you before, Maddy?"

She spun to face him, her mouth open, but the words refused to come out. Madeline stared at him. "How did you..." she trailed off, fear and fury churning in her gut.

"I am smarter than you give me credit." He took a step closer. "You are easy to read, lass. 'Tis not hard to put the two together. When you watch him, your face betrays everything."

"It does not," she pressed her hands to her flaming cheeks. "He told you."

"Aye." Angus grinned. "But I had to beat it out of him."

"You did not," she said in disbelief. "Angus, you did not strike him, did you?" She clutched his broad shoulders and shook him. "Where is he?"

"*Dinnea fash yersel*, Kitten." He placed his hands on her arms, assuring her she need not worry. "He is still here, alive and well. I promise you. I have not killed him, yet."

"Yet," she parroted, her brogue thickening. "If you harm him, Angus Joseph Campbell, I will not be held responsible for my actions."

"And if he kisses you again, Madeline, I will cut his lips off." Angus laughed when she jerked from his grasp. "You never answered my question." She glared at him, but he pressed on anyway, heedless of her glacial stare. "Has he kissed you before?"

"That is none of your concern," she snapped at him. He stepped forward, his hand cradling her chin.

"I love you. I want you to be happy. But I will not let him take advantage of you."

"Alexander has been a gentleman from the beginning of our acquaintance," she replied, defending both herself and the man who stole her heart. "He would never take advantage of me."

"Aye," Angus said on an exhale. "You would know." He pulled her into his embrace. "Guard yourself. Tell me if you have any troubles." He pressed a kiss to her head and then turned to leave.

"Angus," she said softly. He glanced over his shoulder at her. "I thank you, for your concern."

"'Tis my duty," he said, and with those words, he left her.

Madeline tidied up her room, losing herself in the mundane task. As she made her way down to search for Heather, she remembered Angus' question. *Has he kissed you before?*

Nay, she thought with regret. A memory surfaced of a man shrouded in shadows who stole a kiss in the moonlit garden. Would she ever know who dared such a thing? Madeline sighed.

Perhaps it was best for him and that kiss to remain a secret, for stolen kisses are always the sweetest and, by far, the most dangerous.

Chapter Six

The hills outside the keep came alive with the sparkling of firelight and the raucous laughter of men deep in their cups. Alexander built a small fire outside his tent and sat with a flagon of ale, which Angus had graciously provided. Staring into the firelight, Alexander lost himself in the flames. The sound of drunken revelry shook him from his musings. He never drank to excess. If he ever succumbed to the sweet embrace of wine or ale, it would severely hinder his abilities. It would lure him with its intoxicating kiss and strangle the life from him. He had seen it happen too many times before to not be careful.

Alexander acknowledged a few men as they walked past his fire. They nodded, raising their cups in salute as they stumbled past. He shook his head. These men would never accept him as one of them. He was involved in a mummers farce now.

With a sigh, he reclined against the small woodpile. Once again, he had been foolish enough to embroil himself in another man's personal affairs. He should have just been grateful the laird had not taken the truth in a bad way. He seemed to take the news in stride, using it to his best advantage, which was both wise and suspicious in Alexander's opinion.

"Care if I join you?" Angus' voice came out of the shadows. The man had an uncanny ability to sneak up on people. He moved as a cat would, weaving through the darkness, watching and waiting for unsuspecting prey. He proved to be gregarious and mischievous, much like Gabriel. The fleeting thought of his brother made him frown. Alexander gestured for Angus to sit.

"You look as though you could use some company." Angus pulled the stopper from his flagon and took a healthy swallow. "Not much for conversation, are you?"

He knew the other man was attempting to be his friend, but it had been so long since Alexander allowed anyone close enough, he was unsure if he remembered the way of it.

"Nay," Alexander replied. "My brother complains constantly I am too serious." He laughed, but it sounded more like a snort. "Gabriel had been blessed with the golden tongue, not I."

"How many siblings do you have?" Angus asked, leaning forward.

"Two brothers and two sisters," he said, not turning his attention from the flames. "My sisters live with my mother still, unless they have married."

"You have not seen them in some time, have you?"

"Nay," Alexander said, closing his eyes. "A visit home is long overdue."

"And your brothers?"

"Safe behind English stone, if God be gracious," he said, a sad tone weaving through his reply.

Angus glanced at the clear skies. Alexander followed suit, admiring the sparkling of light in the heavens, a canvas of black and blues twinkling with gemstones. He always enjoyed the night, the darkness. It probably held over from his time as the Shadow Guardian.

Perhaps he could get information another way, slipping into the hood led to all forms of knowledge if utilized properly. His lip quirked at the thought of kissing Madeline again in the moonlight, beneath the anonymity of the shadow's garb. He had no need for it to achieve such an end. He merely had to tell her the truth, if she had not surmised as much after his actions earlier. *Why must it be so damnably hard to say what one felt?* He shook his head.

"Something amuses you?" Angus asked.

"Aye," Alexander said. "Me, being here. I do not belong. They all know it." He swung his arm wide, gesturing to the camp. "On the morrow, I shall make a fool of myself."

"Can you fight with a blade?"

"Aye," Alexander replied.

"Can you shoot a bow?"

"Aye."

"Are you able to hold your own?"

"What are you trying to say, Angus?" Alexander said, frustrated by everything.

"You are a knight, by God. You have trained for this since you were a lad. 'Tis in your blood." Angus spoke, impassioned. "You have one advantage over the lot of them. You are not quick to anger. That will be where the rest of them fail. But I warn you, if you want to convince them you are worthy of my sister, then you will have to show them you will take none of their shite. Not from any of them. And they will test you, trust me."

"You wish for me to start a fight?" Alexander asked wanting to be sure he heard Angus correctly.

"They will test you. 'Tis how you react that will determine the amount of respect they will pay you." Angus emptied his flagon in one swallow and stood. "Best get your rest. Dawn comes early in the highlands."

"Aye," he said as he watched the man disappear into the shadows.

Alexander stood, brushed the dirt and leaves from his clothes, and disappeared into his tent. If there was one thing he knew how to do, it was fight. A friendly competition would prove nothing compared to the intense heat and danger of true combat. He was a trained knight, who avoided tournaments at all cost. Memories of all the contests he had observed reared in the back of his mind.

He would do it for Madeline, all of it. He curled up on the feather pallet and stared at the wavering cloth of the tent overhead. Much later, he finally drifted to sleep, determined to do his very best.

Alexander woke unable to breathe. He wrenched his eyes open, meeting a curious, sprightly face peering down into his own.

"May I aid you in some way, my lady?" he said, recognizing Madeline's sister, Heather. The child sat astride his chest. Then he felt it…the cold kiss of steel against his neck. *What the devil?* Her hand clutched a dagger pressed to his throat.

"You made my sister cry," she whispered, her sweet voice holding a deadly threat. "I will kill you if you hurt her again."

"My lady," he said, his voice low. "It was not my intention to make your sister cry, nor do I have any intention bringing harm to her or your any other member of your family." He pressed his finger to the blade, pushing it away from his throat.

Reluctantly she dropped the blade to her side. Alexander breathed a sigh of relief even though she remained perched on his chest. He snatched the blade from her hand and tossed it to the other side of the tent. His hands wrapped around her tiny waist, and he lifted her off him, setting her on the ground. He stood as she scrambled backward, searching for her blade.

"Do you make this a habit then, greeting your guests this way?" He waved a finger at her. "I should tell your father what you are about."

The girl stood. Dressed in a blue and red tartan gown, she straightened her spine and tucked her dagger back into the sheath in her bodice.

"Tell him; he will not believe you," she said tossing her wild hair over her shoulder. She had spirit this one, wild and untamed like the highland hills.

"But he will believe me." A voice echoed from the tent entrance. "And he will tan your arse, wee hellion. How many times have I told you to mind your manners?" Angus stormed into the tent. "You need to learn to be a lady. Mayhap, I should tell Madeline. She would straighten you right quick."

Heather stuck her tongue out at him and stormed into the morning light, leaving Alexander and Angus gaping after her.

"My pardon for her, Alexander," Angus apologized. "She is a wild thing who needs a firm motherly figure in her life. A house full of men is no place for a lady. I am afraid she has picked up some bad habits."

Alexander could not have agreed more. He snatched his sword from next to the bed and fastened it around his waist. "Have you come to terrorize me as well, before I have even broken my fast?"

"Of course," Angus said as he clapped his hand on Alexander's shoulder. "Come, you have a long day ahead, 'tis wise you eat."

The duo left the tent and headed for the great hall. Alexander inhaled, calming himself. He hated tournaments. The bluster and showmanship never failed to grate on his nerves, one of the reasons he did not compete in the baron's spring tournament. He trained hard to be an efficient knight. Alexander had no reason to have to prove his abilities to anyone. He needed neither the gold nor the glory, considering it a waste of time. Today, he would lay his opinion aside and step into the ring. This tournament held more importance than any other for the prize held far more value to him than he cared to admit to anyone. He sighed.

As they entered the bailey, Alexander caught a glimpse of Heather sitting on the fence near the stables. Her gaze followed him, narrowing as she squinted against the morning sun. He would have to speak to Madeline about her little sister. The girl had far too much spirit to be left to her own devices. Hopefully Madeline would be able to provide a better direction for her as she grew.

Once inside, Alexander's stomach grumbled at the scent of the morning meal. He helped himself to some oat porridge, a few pieces of meat, and a crusted piece of bread.

"You might want to just pack your stuff, southerner." The snide comment came from behind him. Alexander turned to face the man.

"You are not welcome here," the highlander added, spitting on the floor. He stood roughly Alexander's height, with the bulk to match. His hair shone black as a raven's wing, pulled back into a long tail fastened with a leather strap at the base of his neck. A long scar ran along his neck, disappearing in the top of his shirt.

"I do not believe that decision is yours to make, lad," Alexander replied, returning to his meal.

"Who are you callin' lad?" the highlander grabbed a handful of Alexander's shirt.

"Och now, enough. There will be no brawling in my house!" The laird's voice boomed over the din in the great hall. "I will not have petty rivalries. Douglas, rein your boy in, or I shall not allow him to compete."

With a snarl, the Douglas heir released Alexander's plaid. "Watch yourself. Would not want you to get hurt or muss your pretty hair." He left the hall, followed by three other brawny men.

Alexander turned to the laird, who engaged in a heated conversation with another older man, presumably the head of the Douglas clan. He sat at the nearest table and began to eat. Although he had dealt with men like Douglas before, never had Alexander wanted to react out of impulse. He took several calming breaths, forcing himself to focus on the end goal, not exposing himself in a fit of rage. Several of the other competitors eyed him from their seats. Quickly finishing his meal, he stood and left the hall, overwhelmed with the desire to get some fresh air.

Alexander stepped into the courtyard and scanned the people milling about, searching for Madeline. Not finding her, he walked down to the field where preparations were being made for the tournament.

The open space highlighted by the blue skies and rolling hills had greened from the recent rains. There were no ornate decorations or fancy banners. All the clans displayed their flags proudly on their tents where they mingled among the vendors selling their wares. It acted as a social event as well as an economic one. Alexander grinned. It seemed the laird realized the importance of such an event in his village when it came to their economic strength.

"'Tis beautiful, is it not?" Madeline said approaching from the direction he had just come. She glanced down at her hands, knotted in her skirts. They walked together toward the loch, finding a shaded spot beneath the canopy of trees.

"Is there something wrong, my lady?" he asked, reaching for her but pulling his hand back at the last moment. She glanced up at him.

"I wanted to apologize," she said. "For Heather. Angus told me what she did to you this morn." Her face flushed pink, framed by loose tendrils of her golden streaked hair. A vision of loveliness set against the loch and the shadowed forest, she stole his breath away.

He cleared his throat. "No need to apologize. Your sister is merely concerned for your wellbeing. 'Tis her way of protecting you."

"But," she said as she stepped forward. "She could have hurt you." Madeline reached out and caressed his cheek, running her fingertips across the scruff on his jaw.

"Your concern is touching," he replied, taking her hand in his. "But as you can see, I have escaped unharmed."

"This time." Heather interrupted their moment.

Alexander dropped Madeline's hand as her sister wedged her body between them, effectively pushing them apart. Heather turned and faced Alexander, her hands on her tiny hips. The determined look on her face reminded him of a cross between Madeline and Evelyn, and it truly terrified him. Such a combination could be deadly, especially to the man who fell in love with her. He felt a stab of pity for the poor fool.

"Heather!" Madeline scolded her sister, taking her by the hand and dropping down on one knee to meet her sister face to face. "Why must you threaten Alexander?"

"He has come to take you away, and you have only just arrived." The girl pouted, and her lip trembled as she held Madeline's gaze. "Take me along. I beg of you." Her words were barely above a whisper.

His heart ached at her plea. Two stories he heard today from little Heather, and he believed both of them. She needed her sister desperately. He could see the love in her gaze mingled with tears.

"Heather," he said as he kneeled. "Come here." She glanced at him, as if unsure of what he would do. She hesitated for a moment but then stepped closer. He placed his hand in hers. "I promised I would not hurt your sister. The promise extends to you as well. If I win your sister's hand, you may come with her.

As long as it is agreeable to your father."

The girl's face brightened, her tear filled eyes blinking rapidly. "Truly?" She squealed when he nodded, throwing her arms around Alexander's neck. He rocked back on his heels, stunned by her reaction, but he embraced her. Madeline watched, her hand at her throat, close to tears.

Oh, saints preserve me, do not cry. I do not know what to do with a weeping woman. Alexander pleaded in his mind.

Heather released him and turned to her sister, hugging her. "I hope you win, Alexander." She grinned at him and then bounded up the hill toward the keep.

"You are competing?" Madeline asked as he rose to his feet.

"Aye," he said, meeting her narrowed gaze.

"Why?"

"Your brother invited me to join in the festivities."

"Is that the only reason?" Madeline stepped closer and traced the pattern of the brooch over his heart. She slid her hand up and around his neck.

"Madeline, what are you doing?" Alexander's gaze darted to the field surrounding them. If they would be seen such, he would be torn to bits by his fellow competitors. He would be seen as a threat to all the other men by claiming what had not been officially won. She persisted, her hands pulling him toward her.

"I am thanking you properly," she whispered, as she pressed a kiss to his lips. Soft and warm, Madeline wove a spell with just a touch. Her fingers toyed with his hair, pulling and twirling it between her fingers. When she pulled away, her gold-flecked hazel eyes sparkled with a hundred promises.

"I have not won yet," Alexander said.

"You do not need to win anything, *mo chride*," she murmured. With a breath, she pulled away, leaving him to watch her return to the keep.

He pondered what she said. *What did she call me?* He had heard those words before. Heading in the direction of the tents, the memory hit him. His mother had said those words to his father every day. *My heart.* Alexander stopped, stunned by the realization: Madeline loved him.

Chapter Seven

Madeline sat in the seat of honor next to her father on the stand overlooking the tournament field. Her attention shifted to the one man who stood apart from the rest. Alexander leaned over the water barrel and splashed the cool liquid over his face. It soaked his clothes. His mahogany hair shone with copper highlights as he ran his fingers through it. He had no family cheering him on, only the full force of the rival clans taunts and jeers. Alexander had not even flinched at their barbed words and vicious slights. They heckled him for being a lowlander. Every time, he would meet her gaze, then return to the task at hand.

The sun rested at the highest point in the sky. A trickle of sweat slid between her breasts. Madeline fanned herself with her hand. A servant approached, offering her a cup of refreshing wine. She took it and drank deeply, letting the cool, sweet liquid soothe her dry throat.

As she sat back in her seat, the clash of steel broke her distracted thoughts. A pair of suitors faced off on the field. Mackenzie stood fighting a Stewart. They circled each other, and then attacked. A slash from Mackenzie deflected off Stewart's blade.

Madeline rolled her eyes. This had been her father's solution to finding her a suitor. Having them hack, slash, and pummel each other into the ground until one was left standing? She now realized how sane Evelyn had been in her opinions concerning women and their right to decide their own future. And whether or not her decision included a man.

They labored under the delusion they would win her heart with this farce. She laughed. All of them, in their grass and blood stained tartans, could no more become lords of English land than win her heart with their ridiculous tournament. Madeline looked at her father, his face impassive as one hand stroked his gray-tinted beard.

"Are you not enjoying the festivities, lass?" he asked. She blinked and returned her gaze to the fight before them.

"Aye, Father," she replied sweetly, taking another sip of wine.

"You always were a terrible liar." He chuckled as he leaned toward her. "Do you not trust me, lass? I ken you have been away for a long while, but..." She placed her hand on his arm, and he fell silent.

"I do trust you, Father," she said, patting his arm.

Stewart received a hard blow, knocking him to the ground. He threw his hands up, yielding, as Mackenzie's blade hovered at his throat.

"Duncan Mackenzie wins the bout," a man cried out. A rouse of cheers and curses rippled through the crowd as the men left the field.

"Alexander Kerr," the same man called, "fighting Willem Douglas." Madeline's hand trembled slightly, her grip tightened on the cup.

"Ah, now this should be entertaining," her father said, reclining in his chair. "More wine." A servant handed him a goblet, and he took it, his gaze riveted on the two men stepping into the ring.

She watched Alexander face Douglas. While Alexander held his sword steady before him, Douglas brandished his in a gaudy attempt to garner cheers from the crowd. *Showmanship, all in vain.* Madeline remembered Evelyn laughing at knights who performed such an extravagant dance. They believed it intimidated their opponent, but in reality it only expended energy, causing the fighter to tire quickly and putting him at a disadvantage. She allowed herself a small smile. Alexander's odds increased with every superfluous movement his opponent made.

Douglas brought the broadsword down in a swinging arc. Alexander deflected it with his blade, stepping out with his right foot. The men circled a few paces, their eyes locked. Madeline held her breath, afraid even a single one would change the balance between the men.

Douglas stepped forward, thrusting his sword toward

Alexander's chest. With a twist of the hilt, Alexander blocked it, bringing his elbow up and shoving Douglas back. They stumbled apart. Douglas looked murderous, his long black hair pulling free from the leather tie. He bared his teeth and took a wild swing at Alexander, who spun out of the blade's reach then circled around Douglas.

Madeline partook in another drink, hoping it would fortify her. The men faced off again. A myriad of thrusts, parries, a few disgruntled attempts to hack a limb off, and then in a flash Alexander caught the edge of Douglas' tartan with his blade, twisted it in the material and pulled, ripping the plaid. The highlander gripped the hilt of his sword with both hands and brought the broadsword down, aiming for a slash across Alexander's chest.

Madeline shut her eyes. She cringed at the clang of steel against steel. When she opened them, Alexander had his blade blocking the other as it inched closer toward him. With a hard shove, he pushed Douglas back. Alexander brought his sword up in a flash and held the steel tip against Douglas' neck before the other man could raise his weapon.

The spectators cheered, surprised by the lowlander and his swordplay. A hush then fell over the crowd as Alexander spoke, his blade pressing against his opponent's throat. "Yield?"

She saw the fury in the other man's expression, the hatred Douglas bore Alexander. He would never yield. Douglas stepped back and threw his sword down, but he never said a word.

The crowd cheered again. Several of the men clapped Alexander on the shoulder as he exited the ring.

Douglas, like a chastised child, snatched up his sword and stomped off the field, a handful of his men at his heels. Madeline allowed herself a sigh of relief.

Angus approached Alexander, handing him a flagon. He pulled the stopper and took a long drink. As he lowered it, he glanced at her. A half smile touched his lips. The moment shattered as Angus drew him into the crowd.

As the next two men geared up for their bout, she watched Alexander disappear into the crowd with her brother. Madeline would never be able to concentrate after that. She tampered down the desire to chase after him and forced herself to turn her attention back to the contestants on the field.

The afternoon wore on. Bout after bout, Alexander put his opponents to shame. It came as no surprise to her when her father named him champion of the sword. Archery would be the second event. Excusing herself, she returned to the keep to freshen up.

Heather sat perched on the keep wall when Madeline entered the bailey.

"What in the bloody hell are you doin' up there?" she yelled, not curtailing the curse as it left her lips. "Get down here this moment!"

Heather slowly climbed down from her perch. When her feet were planted firmly on the ground, Madeline rushed to her side.

"What were you doing up there?" she asked, checking Heather's hands for cuts or scratches. "You are not a cat, my love. You could have fallen." Madeline's brogue thickened as the fear bubbled inside of her. "What would I do if something happened to you?"

Heather hugged her. Just wrapped her arms around Madeline's neck and clung to her. After a few moments, Heather backed away.

"I like climbing," Heather said simply, as if it explained everything.

"'Tis not ladylike," Madeline replied, giving her a motherly look of disapproval. "We have discussed this already. You cannot continue this behavior. You are a lady, 'tis important you start behaving like one."

"Why?" Heather cocked her head like a confused hound.

"'Tis the way of the world." Madeline sighed. Heather asked a valid question, but, sadly, she had no answer to satisfy the girl other than the platitudes that had been offered to her since her own childhood. Living with her cousin had taught her much, but it still provided her with no answers. She tugged on the tangled curl escaping from her sister's haphazard braid.

"I know not why the world is the way it is, my love. Come," Madeline said, taking Heather by the hand. "Let us cool off. I shall fix your braid, then we shall return together and watch the archery competition." The little girl smiled up at her.

The tent felt a bit cooler, and Alexander sat down, grateful to be away from the masses of people. He truly hated these events. It never bothered him when he stood off to the side watching as one of the crowd, but participating always made him uncomfortable. Gabriel used to tease him about his penchant for hiding amongst the banners, avoiding the crowds.

Angus sat down across from him. "I thought Douglas would lop your head off for a moment," he said, taking a swig from the flagon. "You got a wee bit of luck on your side."

"Luck had naught to do with it," Alexander said dryly. "The man fights with his anger at the front. It makes him predictable and prone to mistakes."

"Aye, you may be right," Angus replied, pointing a finger at Alexander. "But I was talking about him stabbing you in the back when you tanned his arse." He chuckled, pressing the drink to his lips again.

"Why would he hate me so much?" Alexander said. "I have taken nothing from him."

"Not yet."

Alexander sighed. They all competed for Madeline's hand after all. Why should it surprise him a man slighted in mock combat would harbor such hate toward him? He shook his head. The temper raging inside of Douglas could prove to be a problem later if he refused to be careful. Alexander would be sure to offer him a token of peace, hoping to stave off any threats which might arise from the tournament. Some men simply did not like to lose. They have no stomach for it, and in their blind rage, they do stupid things.

"You are wise, my friend," Alexander said, offering a hunk

of bread to Angus, who accepted it.

"Do not tell my father," Angus joked. "He still does not believe I do anything but make jests all the time. I would hate for him to get the wrong impression of me." A sly grin crossed his lips.

"You would get along quite nicely with my brother," Alexander said.

"Why is that?" Angus' eyes danced with mirth.

"You both laugh too much, and jest at the most inopportune moments."

"My comedic timing is near legendary," Angus said, acting indignant.

"You both bray like a jackass in need of a good thrashing."

Both men broke into throaty laughter.

"How are you with a bow?" Angus asked as the laughter died down.

"Fairly accurate, most of the time," Alexander replied. He was not nearly as good as Gabriel, but they both trained with the weapon enough to hit a mobile as well as sedentary target. His mind replayed the archery lesson with Madeline the day before. The feel of her against him as she tensed pulling the bowstring taut would be forever branded in his mind. He had almost kissed her then, the sweet smell of her hair, the softness of her skin. It called to him, luring him closer, making him forget himself.

"What about heavy lifting?" Angus question snapped him from his reverie. The enticing memory popped like a soap bubble. He glanced at Madeline's brother, afraid he knew the direction of his thoughts.

"Heavy lifting? What does that have to do with the tournament?" Alexander asked, concerned he had missed something along the way.

"One of the events will be the caber toss." Angus' grin grew steadily as he watched Alexander.

He had forgotten one of the main events in Scottish tournament involved the measure of strength by tossing large tree trunks. He groaned. "Ah," he said running his hand through his hair. "Mayhap ale or angels had removed that particular event from my memories."

Angus laughed. "Well, you better practice before the event then," he said, standing. "There is a small clearing in the woods were I used to play as a child. I could take you there and show you how 'tis done."

"I may take you up on your offer." Alexander stood, shaking out his plaid. He was a solid archer and a steady, efficient swordsman, but he had not trained for feats of strength. The highland tournament was a test of endurance, strength, and skill. Alexander believed he might have a fighting chance of winning if he could place in all of the events.

"By the by, how does your father choose the winner?" Alexander asked as they walked from the tent. The sun warmed him. He squinted against it. "I mean, what if the same man does not win every challenge?"

Angus nodded. "He awards marks based on your performance and how many challengers you have gone up against. Ultimately it will be his decision and no one else's."

"Will it not put him in an uncomfortable position with some of the clansmen if they do not like his choice?"

"Aye," Angus said, glancing at him. "I would not wish to be in his shoes when he makes his decision."

Alexander agreed. He often found he received the ire of most people who opposed the choice when they discovered he had made the decision. It very seldom made him friends. Gabriel would say it his charming personality won him the love of those around him. Though, he never believed the joke amusing. Not everyone could live freely, without giving consideration to the consequences of their actions.

The duo walked toward the fields again, the sun dipping in the sky.

Once the archery contest ended, they would meet in the great hall. A feast was being prepared to bolster the spirits of the defeated and keep the spirit of revelry alive. Alexander had a feeling more than one fight would break out during the night from too much drink mixed with wounded pride.

A tall, quiet man in gray and brown plaid stood leaning

against the outer wall of the keep. He watched them from beneath hooded lids. Alexander had noticed him around the camp. He kept the company of his fellow clansmen, quiet and observant. A man of few words, not that Alexander could blame him. He understood all too well the desire to keep to oneself.

"Good fight today, McLairn," Angus said as they approached him. McLairn offered a half smile and stepped forward to greet them.

"Och, 'twas nothing. I would have won the bout had MacDonald not caught me with his wild swing and an elbow to the jaw," he said, rubbing the sore spot with his hand.

Alexander agreed. The unconventional blow by MacDonald's sword caught McLairn unaware. While it had not been intentional, it certainly offered him an advantage and allowed him to win the bout.

MacDonald had underestimated Alexander and was relieved of his weapon within seconds. Too blinded by his pride and not willing to learn from observing the first two men Alexander had beaten. McLairn, on the other hand, saw everything. He quickly mimicked his opponents' moves and proved even quicker in anticipating them. The man had taken the defeat with a good attitude and sat watching the rest of the tournament with intense scrutiny.

McLairn turned his attention to Alexander. He nodded. "You have quite a skill with your sword, Kerr. 'Tis a shame I did not get to test your abilities on the field today."

"Aye," Alexander agreed. "Facing you would have been a welcome challenge."

"Perhaps we shall meet again," he replied with a smooth confidence. "I beg pardon." He broke away from them. "My lady, you are a vision of perfection."

Alexander turned. McLairn had intercepted Madeline who was leaving the keep. He offered his arm. She slipped her arm in his and glanced over her shoulder at Angus and Alexander. Her smile hit him harder than any blow he had ever received in combat. She returned her gaze to the man by her side. A pang of jealousy shot through him.

"You look like you are about to hit something," Angus said.

Alexander shook his head and squared his shoulders. "'Tis nothing."

"Och, you are full of shite." Angus clapped a hand on his shoulder. "Come, you can win her favor and put the poor bastard to shame."

"You truly believe your sister would be happiest with me?" Alexander asked, unsure why he was spilling his guts to a stranger. A stranger who reminded him of his brother. He sighed. "I just want her to be happy. If it means she marries another, then so be it."

"Alexander." Angus' voice turned serious. "I watched her pine after you for days when I brought her north. I saw tenderness in her expression when she saw you in the great hall the first night." He paused. "She loves you. So far you have proven yourself to be an honorable man, a decent friend, and a wicked swordsman. Hell, I would marry you if I could." He chuckled. "If you love her, do not give up yet."

Alexander laughed. "You are a wise man." They began walking again. "And it would make your father proud if he knew it."

"The old man would never believe you."

Alexander shook his head. He hoped he could do this. The memory of a certain golden-haired lass and an impromptu archery lesson made his body ache for release.

Chapter Eight

The mood in the keep fluttered with merriment. Rivalries were put aside for the meal to be resumed the next day on the fields. Madeline sat next to her father and brothers, enjoying the delicious food and sweet red wine. The tables were full, near to bursting with a dozen clans and their families. Her father rose from his seat and mingled with his guests, taking time to greet everyone and share stories.

Madeline's cheeks hurt from smiling. The men competing for her affections in the tournament offered her tokens of their esteem and flowery words. She smiled and accepted their compliments. Her attention strayed from them, constantly searching for Alexander. He had not appeared for the feast, and she became more concerned as the hour grew later. Glancing at the end of the table, she noticed Angus' absence as well.

The musician played a lively tune complimented by the sounds of laughter and conversation. Madeline excused herself and headed for the kitchen. Heather always ate with the cook. They were thick as thieves, those two. The cook was a plump woman near Madeline's father's age and the closest thing to a mother figure Heather had.

Heather had not been lying when she said she did as she pleased. It seemed as though Heather had become the eyes and ears of the keep. Knowing her sister saw and heard everything happening inside these stone walls shocked Madeline. Her cheeks flared red when Heather had confessed to overhearing amorous encounters and arguments. Madeline asked her sister to cease all eavesdropping and behave like a proper lady. She had promised, but old habits were hard to break.

Heather sat on the table, nibbling on a tart when Madeline entered the kitchen.

"Good eve, my lady. Are you enjoying the feast?" the cook asked, glancing up from her pastries.

"Everything is splendid, and the food is delicious. You have outdone yourself," Madeline replied with a smile.

"Why are you down here then?" Heather piped up, a smear of fruit jam on her nose and flour on her cheeks. Her hair hung loose again. Madeline sighed. The girl would be the death of her.

"Have you seen Alexander?" she asked the wee hellion.

"Aye," she replied then stuffed the rest of the pastry into her mouth. Her puffed cheeks made her words near incomprehensible when she continued. "Thewehn wtoe thweo foswnet..." Crumbs spilled from her lips.

"Swallow your food before you answer." Madeline tapped her foot and waited.

Heather swallowed the mouthful and wiped her mouth on the back of her hand. "He went into the forest with Angus." She shrugged. "They left right before the feast began."

The meal had been going on for the last several hours. "Where did they go exactly?"

Heather jumped down from the table. "Come," she said, stuffing three tarts into her pockets before snatching Madeline's hand. "I will show you." Before she could object, Heather dragged her from the kitchen and into the warm night air. "Best if we ride," she added, heading for the stables. "Can you still ride?"

"For your information, a lady can ride." Madeline sniffed. "They can shoot and carry a sword as well."

Heather stopped in her tracks and spun around facing Madeline, her hands on her hips. "You have secrets! I knew it!" She lunged at her sister, wrapping her arms around her waist. "You can tell me all about them on the way." Releasing her, Heather resumed her determined stride toward the stables.

"How far is this place?" Madeline chased after her.

"Just over the ridge, into the forest, near the far side of the loch," Heather replied. Within moments, they had saddled and mounted their horses, leaving the keep through the postern gate. The sun was setting, casting long shadows as they rode over the hill.

The forest seemed familiar. Madeline vaguely remembered

playing here as a child while her brothers and father hunted. The sun lingered on the horizon with a bloody grip. Red fingers of light reached through the trees. She glanced at Heather, who rode beside her. Neither of them had spoken since they entered the woods.

"There is a clearing just around the bend," Heather said, urging her mount ahead of Madeline's. A shout echoed through the trees. Madeline nudged her horse faster, catching up to Heather. They entered the clearing and reined their horses to a stop.

Angus stood to the side of Alexander, who was bent over at the waist, his hands on his hips. He threw his head back, his face drenched with sweat, his hair soaked. He pushed it back as he turned to Angus. They were in conversation and did not notice the horses entering the glen.

"Angus!" Heather shouted, waving her arms. "What are you doin' out here?"

Angus and Alexander glanced up. They slowly made their way to where the horses stood. "One could say the same for you, wee hellion. Have you come spying again?"

"Heather was good enough to lead me to you. You were missed at the feast. Father inquired after you both," Madeline lied, sliding from the saddle. "You did well in the archery contest." She looked at Alexander. "Second place is better than last."

"Aye," he said with a nod. His last shot had been a fraction farther from the bull's-eye than McLairn's. A hair of difference won him the honor of runner up. "I thank you kindly, my lady."

"Come now," she said. "McLairn is the best archer in Scotland." Madeline laid her hand on his arm. "Are you two hiding from the other competitors?"

Alexander pursed his lips and glanced at Angus.

"Teaching Alexander how to toss a caber." Angus shrugged as he opened his flagon and drank.

"You never..." Madeline drifted off. "Nay, I guess you would never have done that before." She brightened. "Have you accomplished anything productive in your stolen moments away?" Her hand still rested on his arm, his skin hot through his damp shirt. His arm pulsed beneath her touch.

"I think I have the basics worked out," he said, a smile tugging at his lips. "The sun has set. Shall we return to the keep?"

"Aye," Angus said, clapping his hands together. "I am famished." He pulled himself up into the saddle behind Heather. "We walked," he explained, wheeling the horse around.

"I can walk," Alexander said.

"You will not," Madeline said in a stern voice. "You seem as though you are about to collapse. Fighting all day, working into the darkness. I insist you ride." She put her hands on her hips.

He opened his mouth as if to argue with her but shook his head instead. "You are as stubborn as Evelyn."

Madeline blinked rapidly, surprised by his familiar use of her cousin's name. "You mean Lady Evelyn?"

"Aye," he said. "Lady Evelyn."

He pulled himself into the saddle and then offered his hand down to her. She placed her hand in his and he lifted her across his lap with ease. The horse danced under the weight, but he nudged it forward to follow Heather and Angus. Madeline swayed against his chest. One hand fisting in his plaid while the other wrapped around his waist in an attempt to steady herself. She glanced at him. His expression seemed blank.

A pang of jealousy shot through her at the thought of Alexander and Evelyn speaking in such familiar terms with each other. With the sun finally set, the light hues of darkness crested the sky. The starlight twinkled overhead as the moon cast enough light for them to follow the trail. In a couple days, it would be full, bright and beautiful. The gentle rocking motion of the horses' pace lulled her into a comfortable position in Alexander's arms. He kept one arm around her body while her head nestled against his chest. She heard the steady pounding of his heart.

"Madeline," he said, breaking the silence. "Why did you come looking for us this eve? The laird could have sent anyone to fetch us to the meal. Why did you take the task upon yourself?"

Dare she tell him the truth? She missed the sound of his voice, his handsome face, the way he made her feel comfortable just with his presence in the room.

"I admit to being concerned," she admitted. "Douglas seemed displeased with you after his defeat, and I overheard some of the other competitors jesting about what color a lowlander would bleed." She held him tighter. "I wanted to be sure you were well." Madeline pondered for a moment then confessed. "And I grew weary of the stares in the great hall."

A rumble of quiet laughter bubbled from deep in his chest. She glanced up at him. He met her gaze. "Not interested in being the center of attention? Those men are desperate to woo you, Madeline. You dismissing their ardent attentions must have stung their pride."

"Not as much as their simpering attempts to win my favor have crippled mine," she replied sharply. "One of them offered me a lock of his own hair!" She shook her head. "'Tis not me they want. They want what my father can offer them with our union. I am merely the prized broodmare to fill their house with heirs."

Alexander remained silent, his embrace tightened around her. Not much, but she noticed his body stiffen at her words.

"I am merely a possession to be bartered and traded." She sighed. "Evelyn was right. 'Tis not fair." She wiggled against him, trying to find a more comfortable seat.

"Madeline," he groaned. "Do not do that."

"What?" she asked innocently, glancing at his face. He had drawn his lower lip between his teeth, his eyes had drifted closed. She released his shirt and touched his unshaven cheek. The rough prickle of new beard scratched her palm.

"Cease your torture, lass," he said, his voice hoarse and breaking.

"Am I hurting you?" She shifted again, bracing her hand on his thigh. His hand tightened on her waist.

"Stop. Moving." He grounded out the words.

"I do not mean to hurt you," she said, sympathetic. She truly had no idea what she did to cause him pain.

"If you would stop your wiggling," he rasped out. She pulled away from him in an effort to give him some space. Madeline slipped, nearly tumbling from the horse when he caught her, his palm cradling her breast. She felt the heat of his hand through the fabric of her gown. A knot formed in the pit of her stomach, twisting and pulling, threatening to tear her apart. She gasped and grasped his plaid to steady herself again. As soon as she settled, his hand released her, resuming its grip on her side.

"My apologies, my lady," he said as their mount climbed the hill toward the keep. Madeline could see Angus and Heather ahead of them, but far enough their words were a whisper on the breeze.

"'Twas my fault I nearly fell," she said, the heat rising in her cheeks.

"I meant for..." He coughed, unable to finish the sentence.

"Oh, that, well," she stammered, her face enflamed. The darkness hid her embarrassment, but it also emboldened her. "I must admit, I liked it."

Alexander said nothing, but his fingertips digging into her side belied his reaction. She felt daring in the moonlight.

"Did you like it as well?" she whispered, her gaze fixed on his face. He bit his lip again. A familiar tingle shot down her spine, landing in the pit of her stomach.

"My lady, 'twas naught but an accident," he replied stiffly. "It will not happen again."

She leaned closer to him, curling against his warm body. "Your touch warms me the way strong wine does. Making me feel weak and helpless and happy, all at once. I cannot help but want more." She reached her hand up to caress his face again. "Would you kiss me again, Alexander?"

Madeline heard his breathing quicken. His heart beat louder beneath her cheek, and his jaw twitched beneath her touch. "You want it as much as I do," she said, feeling wicked and wanton. She had wanted him for so long, to have him so close now and not take a chance seemed wrong.

"I do," he whispered so softly she almost missed his confession.

"Then I am yours." Her breath hitched when he glanced at her, his eyes as dark as the skies above them.

"I cannot," he replied, regret evident in his tone.

"You can," she pleaded. Her body ached for his touch; her lips burned for his kiss. For the past few months she pined for him, forcing herself to be content for the chance of seeing him around the keep. Ever since he kissed her, she knew he wanted her with as much passion as she desired him. Her fingertips journeyed into the soft curls at the nape of his neck, twisting them. "I am at your mercy, Alexander. I beg of you, kiss me."

He muttered a curse before claiming her lips with his own. The kiss made Madeline burn, the pressure building inside as he tasted her. Madeline's arms tightened around him, pulling herself into his heat. She sighed against his mouth.

"Alexander, I..." She stopped abruptly and pulled away from him when she noticed the torches from the keep casting a shadow on his face. They had arrived, and she had been so distracted by him she had not noticed. Madeline pressed her fingers to her lips and straightened as they approached the postern gate. When they entered the bailey, Angus and Heather stood waiting for them.

Angus helped Madeline down from the horse. Alexander dismounted and turned to her.

"Go inside," he said, a tender expression on his normally stoic face. "I shall help Angus with the horses then join you in the great hall."

Madeline nodded.

"Come on," Heather said, taking her by the hand and dragging her inside the door leading to the kitchen. Madeline glanced over her shoulder and saw what she knew in her heart. Alexander was watching her.

Chapter Nine

The tournament started early. The laird wanted to fit the next two events into one day. Alexander swallowed the anxiety roiling in the pit of his stomach. He knew he would never match some of the men when it came to strength. Angus stood next to Madeline and their father. He spied Heather's wild hair as she climbed a nearby tree. He shook his head. A soft spot for Heather had blossomed somewhere along the way. When such an emotion had taken root, he could not hazard a guess.

A shout rang out as Douglas tossed the caber, cheers erupting as it slammed into the dirt flinging clumps of grass into the air. He rubbed his hand over his face and through his hair.

Alexander remembered the first tournament their father had taken them to as lads. Gabriel had laughed and joked the entire time. James took it all very seriously, discussing the finer points of the tournament rules with their father. Alexander observed the bouts, the jousts, and the sparring with a dread in his bones. He hated being the center of attention with all those people watching from the stands, whispering as they passed judgment. He had sworn he would never compete in a tournament for any reason.

"Alexander Kerr," a voice rang out. Alexander stepped forward, pushing away the fear clawing at the back of his throat. The crowd's attention focused on him. He inhaled a deep breath and stepped up to the caber lying on the grass. He squatted and picked it up, lifting with his legs. The weight bore down on him. His muscles quivered from the exertion. Pushing past the pain straining in his legs and arms, he hefted the log into the air with a shout. The log landed with a thud. A round of cheers came up from the crowd. Alexander turned to Angus, who was grinning like a fool, but Madeline's expression stole his breath away. She stood like a lady in her ruby gown, her hands clasped demurely in front of her. The gleam in her eyes sparkled as bright as the sunshine in her golden hair.

Alexander stepped from the ring and walked toward the tent where they stood. He bent over the water barrel and splashed a little on his face and arms.

"Quite impressive," a familiar voice rang behind him. Alexander turned to see McLairn, leaning against a tent pole. His gaze lingered on the next contestant, but his attention remained on Alexander. "It seems you got enough practice last eve?"

"Do you often spy on your competition?" Alexander kept his voice neutral, unsure of the man's intent.

"I take it as a personal duty to know my competition," he said with a slow drawl, his gaze drifting to Alexander. "You have a special interest in Lady Madeline." The words sounded like a statement, not a question. "I have seen the way you look at each other. It would be a shame if someone else won her hand."

"I wish her happiness." Alexander chose his words carefully. "With whoever wins her hand."

McLairn nodded. "As do I." He walked away, disappearing into the crowd.

Alexander stood there, leaning over the barrel, wondering what the man meant by his vague response. Douglas had already taken to harassing him as often as he could. He heard him speaking in not-so-hushed tones earlier while they broke their fast.

Alexander was used to the hushed comments and underhanded insults. Growing up with two brothers gave him thick skin to ward off the taunts of others. He glanced over his shoulder and spotted Douglas heading in his direction, his chest puffed out, black hair glittering like a raven's wing in the sunlight. Bracing himself against the barrel, he splashed another handful of water against his face before turning.

"Kerr." The man sneered as he approached him.

Alexander nodded, pushing his damp hair back from his face. "What do you want?"

"You to leave," Douglas replied without hesitation, pushing Alexander aside and splashing some water on his own face.

"I am not going anywhere." Alexander stepped back. The

man infuriated him with his appalling lack of manners and pompous attitude. He clenched his hands into fists and released, fighting the desire to put the whelp back into his proper place. Douglas could not have been more than a few years younger than Alexander, but it appeared he needed a stiff dose of respect. Alexander had fought enough battles to know humility could, in some cases, be the best form of defense.

"Aye," Douglas said, turning back to face him. "Perhaps you should reconsider." He wiped his face with his hands then smoothed his hair back and tied it with a leather strap. His features reminded Alexander of a bird of prey, his sharp gaze searching for a weakness. Alexander would not give him the satisfaction by betraying even a hint of intimidation. He shuttered his expression and crossed his arms.

"If you are as good as you claim, then how did I beat you during the competition of swords?" Alexander knew better than to taunt him, but he could not stop himself. His fingers itched to teach the cocky bastard a lesson.

"'Twas luck." Douglas' expression darkened as he stepped toward Alexander. He pressed a finger into Alexander's chest. "If I were given a second chance, you would choke on those words."

Alexander stared at him, ignoring the man's touch. The highlander had something to prove and wanted to heal his injured pride. Douglas was baiting him, trying to find a way to get Alexander to bite. His eyes glittered with the promise of a fight. Alexander refused to rise to his challenge. At some point the whelp would find himself at the tip of his blade again if he did not take care to mind his tongue, but now was not that moment.

"You do not have the right to be here, lowlander," he said with disdain. "Lady Madeline deserves a true man in her bed."

Alexander held back the words dancing on his tongue. He wanted to put the imp in his place, teach him a lesson in humility. He opened his mouth when a shout rang above the din of the crowd.

"The winner of the caber toss is Willem Douglas!"

As if the man needed more to bolster his ego, he grinned at Alexander, his expression oozing confidence. He turned and headed for the field to accept his win. A mixture of panic and relief rushed through Alexander. He joined the rest of the contestants as the runner-ups were announced. Alexander graciously accepted second place, and Mackenzie took third.

While they waited for the next event, the guests milled around the tents indulging in the pastries and wine. He caught Madeline's shy glances in his direction. She held her chin high, accepting the attentions of each man in turn. Her voice sounded clear and lovely, like birdsong on a spring day. Alexander waited until she walked away from the gaggle of men vying for her attention and approached her, bowing slightly.

"My lady," he said, offering his arm. "Might you take a turn of the camp with me?"

Madeline smiled and accepted his arm. "Thank you, sir." As they left the hustle of the crowd behind them, she leaned closer, her arm brushing his side. "You did quite well today. Angus is quite pleased with himself."

Alexander glanced at her. "He did not participate."

"Nay, but he did spend time teaching you the proper technique last eve in the forest glen, did he not?" She smiled at him, and he exhaled sharply.

"Aye," he agreed. Had her brother not taken the time to explain the finer points of the sport, he would have certainly failed the day's event. Even the fact he won second place stunned him. "I shall have to offer him a token of my appreciation for his guidance."

Madeline chuckled. "Are you prepared for the next event?"

"I run faster if I am on horseback," he confessed. The fourth event consisted of a foot race through the forest to the other side of the loch and then back to the keep. Alexander prided himself on his fine fighting form, but he had never been known for his speed. Gabriel had always beaten him when they were children. "I fear I may disappoint everyone in this event. My apologies, my lady."

She swayed against him, the scent of roses and cinnamon

tickling his nose. "Do not worry overmuch," she said softly. "I still have faith in you."

He stopped abruptly. "Madeline," he said as she turned to look at him. He ran his free hand through his hair. "Do you still wish to follow through with this? Marrying winner?"

She cocked her head, a hint of sadness in her eyes. "I will do my duty to my family," she replied after a moment of hesitation. "I gave my word. A lady always keeps her word."

He touched her cheek, a soft brush of his fingertips against her skin. "You deserve more than this," he said, unsure of why he said such things. *It feels right.* "You deserve to choose your own fate."

Madeline glanced around. They were alone at the top of the hill overlooking the loch. She sighed, strands of hair blowing in the gentle breeze.

"Och, Alexander," she murmured. "Why could you not have said these things before?" Her gaze met his. "'Tis not so simple now."

"So I have gathered," he replied, tucking the strands of hair behind her ear. "The highland air agrees with you it seems. I have never seen you more lovely."

A blush stole across her cheeks. "It seems to agree with you as well." She laughed. "I have never seen you smile until the night you arrived here."

He had noticed the same problem. Alexander wondered what the difference could be. Angus made him feel at home, even with the knowledge of his family and his true identity. The laird kept his secret close, albeit he had other intentions for Alexander. All the same, he treated Alexander like he did his own sons. Even Heather graced him with a toothy grin whenever she saw him.

But Madeline had garnered the sudden abundance of his smiles. Her quick wit, sharp observations, and unwavering lady-like behavior brought him to his knees. She blossomed here in the mountains of her homeland. While he always considered her attractive, seeing her in her own element amazed him. It brought the roses to her cheeks and the sharp edge to her tongue. *Evelyn would be proud.*

"Shall we return?" she asked, glancing down at the tents cluttered with people. "The next event will be starting soon." He escorted her down the hill without a word, contented to enjoy her silent company.

Angus met them as they reached the tent. "My father would like a word with you, Alexander."

Madeline turned to him. "I thank you for the lovely walk."

He bowed, pressing a kiss to her hand before relinquishing her touch. She blushed and disappeared into the throng of guests. Angus led him to the keep where the laird waited. Alexander pondered the possible reasons for his summons. A knot of dread settled in his stomach.

The laird waited in his presence chamber, staring out the window, when Alexander knocked on the open door.

He turned. "Ah, come in Sir Alexander. Close the door behind you."

Alexander shut the door and then turned to face him. He faced summons like this before, but never had it filled him with apprehension as it did now.

"You requested my presence?"

The older man poured two glasses of Scotch whisky and handed one to Alexander. "I did," he said, sitting down in the chair beside the hearth. "Be seated." He sipped the strong beverage, eyeing Alexander over the rim of the cup.

"I have not uncovered any information to indicate who is stealing from you yet." He sipped the whisky.

"I am certain you will," the laird replied. "However, 'tis not the reason I requested your presence." His expression turned pensive. "I have received news from the capitol. King Robert has died."

Alexander stared at him in disbelief. "You are sure of this information," he asked, leaning forward.

"Aye," he replied, shaking his head. "The news has not yet reached the general population, but it will not be long before it does." He met Alexander's gaze. "This makes your presence here more dangerous. Should they discover your identity, you could be strung up as a spy. I would do everything in my power to stop such a thing from happening, but they will be angry and calling for your blood."

He nodded. Alexander understood when he crossed into Scotland his presence would be unwelcome. Maintaining the charade would be of the utmost importance with the news of King Robert's death hovering over the land. Tensions between the countries would escalate. No doubt the rebels and reivers on the border would increase their activity.

"The tournament will proceed as planned," the laird continued. "I shall make an announcement this evening at the feast. No doubt there will be sentiments expressed which may cause you some discomfort. So I warn you to be on your guard."

"My thanks for imparting this to me." Alexander drank deeply. The news stewed in the pit of his stomach. While his mind told him to return south, his heart told him to stay. The gentle reminder of where his duty lay nagged at him. He pushed the frustrating thoughts away. "Is there anything else?"

"Aye," the older man said, finishing his whisky. "You have done well in the tournament so far, Sir Alexander. It would seem hearty Scottish blood flows through you. Not that I doubted your lineage for a moment, but seeing you in action does present an interesting perspective on what kind of man you truly are."

"Gra'mercy, my laird," he replied, unsure where the conversation was leading.

"Do you play chess?"

"Chess?"

"Aye."

"I was taught the game," Alexander confessed, furrowing his brow. "Though I am afraid I have not played it in years."

"Good," the laird replied, leaning back in his chair. "Would you care to join me after the evening meal for a game?"

"If it is your wish." Alexander swallowed the last of his drink. "Will that be all?"

"Aye, you may go," the laird replied, a smile resting lightly on his lips. "Remember to pace yourself."

"My laird?" Alexander asked, confused by the statement.

"The foot race." The laird's hazel eyes twinkled. "Pace yourself, lad, and you will have no troubles."

Alexander felt the familiar tug at the corners of his mouth. Suppressing it, he stood. "I shall endeavor to heed your advice." He strode from the room, wondering why the laird would trust him with such information. He shook his head and crossed the great hall, heading out into the bailey in search of Angus. He had a race to win.

Chapter Ten

Alexander kept pace with the leaders, taking the laird's advice had gained him a late lead. The bloodcurdling scream that echoed through the silent trees stopped Alexander in his tracks. Turning back, he ran toward the direction of the harrowing scream.

Heather lay in the middle of the path, a large tree branch nearby. Alexander dropped to his knees. *She must have fallen from the tree.*

"Heather. Heather?" he shouted. She lay still, her breathing shallow. He gathered her into his arms and carefully stood. She felt so fragile; her limp body dangled like a rag doll. Alexander's heart constricted. He had to get her help and quickly. The race no longer mattered. With purposeful steps, he made for the keep, clutching her against his chest.

When he broke through the tree line, he noticed the other competitors climbing the hill. Keeping an even pace, he mounted the same hill and then descended toward the keep. His mind raced. She must have been hiding in one of the trees watching the race. He had noticed her penchant for climbing. Madeline had told her a hundred times not to do it, and yet even that had not stopped her. He glanced at her pale face. Alexander hoped she had not done irreparable damage. For the first time since his brother's injury, he prayed.

As he approached the keep, the crowd cheered. When they saw who he carried, a collective gasp rippled through the crowd. Alexander walked directly toward the gates.

"Tell the laird his daughter is injured," he said as he passed through the mass of spectators. "And someone fetch the surgeon and the wise woman," he snapped.

"Alexander!" Madeline's shout stopped him. He turned to face her. When she saw Heather, her hand flew to her mouth as a sob escaped. She rushed to his side. "What happened?"

He shook his head. "I think she fell from a tree," he said. "Where should I put her? She needs a healer."

Madeline nodded. "You can put her in her chamber. Follow me." She walked ahead of him, leading him through the keep. She opened the door to the chamber next to her own. "Put her down gently," she said, moving to the opposite side of the bed.

Alexander laid her down. The girl remained unconscious, her face pale and each breath sounded as though it pained her to draw it. He glanced at Madeline, who began undressing the girl.

"Go fetch my father, along with Old Mary," she said in a calm tone. She paused and looked at him when he did not move. "Alexander," she said, tears slowly pooling in her eyes. "I beg of you, hurry. Go."

Alexander left the room, helplessness enveloping him. He dashed down the stairs and broke into the great hall just as the laird entered from the bailey.

"Where is she?" he said, his breathing labored from rushing to the keep.

"She is in her chamber. Madeline is with her," he said. "I must fetch..." His voice trailed off as an old woman entered the same door as the laird. She held a basket on her arm. Her withered face detracted nothing from the sharp look she gave him.

"Where is the girl? Is she in her bed? Stand aside," she shouted pushing through the men and making for the stairs. She ascended with a pace that belied her age. He turned his attention to the laird again.

The laird shrugged as he followed behind the old woman. "Old Mary," he said over his shoulder as if it explained everything. "I must go to my daughter."

Alexander stood alone in the great hall. He dropped into a chair and leaned forward, burying his face in his hands. It hit him hard, as it had with Gabriel. *Not again.* The memory of lifting his blood-soaked brother in his arms flashed before him. He cringed. *First Gabriel, now Heather.* Alexander was beginning to feel cursed.

A hand settled on his shoulder, startling him. He glanced

up. Angus offered a wary smile and sat down next to him.

"What happened, Alexander?"

"I was running through the forest when I heard a scream." He swallowed, remembering the way his blood froze when he heard the sound. A shiver wracked him. "I went back and found her on the ground. I wondered if she was dead, she lay so still." He closed his eyes.

Angus did not say anything. He sat silently waiting for Alexander to continue the tale.

"She was breathing but unconscious." He pushed on, "I brought her here as fast as I could. I hope..." He stopped, unable to say anything more. It felt as if the world stopped. The only thing that mattered was Heather. He mumbled a silent prayer.

"I thank you for bringing her home," Angus said. "Old Mary knows more than anyone when it comes to healing, and Heather is a strong girl."

Together, they sat in the great hall, waiting for any news of Heather's condition. Silence descended on the duo. A servant brought them a pitcher of ale and a plate of bread, cheese, and cold meat. The food lay untouched, but the ale disappeared long before a word was spoken again.

The sound of heavy footfalls descending the staircase snapped the men to attention. They stood, waiting for some news. The laird stopped before them.

"How is she?" Alexander asked, stepping forward.

"Old Mary says she will live," he said rubbing his hand across his beard. "She has a broken arm. Until she wakes, we cannot be sure what other damage has been done." He sighed.

"For what you did, I thank you," he said, clapping his hand on Alexander's shoulder. "You gave up a chance at victory to help my child. Your kindness will never be forgotten." He walked past them heading for the bailey. "The feast must continue, as must the tournament. I have a duty as host to see to the wellbeing of everyone in my care." He opened the door and stepped outside.

Angus turned to Alexander. "Come," he said. "Let us join him. There is naught we can do up there." He gestured to the stairs.

Alexander nodded. He had a point. They could only wait and pray.

The sunset light shone through the slender window in Heather's chamber. Madeline sat on the bed and dabbed a cool cloth on her sister's forehead. Old Mary had set the girl's broken arm and provided instructions for her recovery. She left with the promise of her return on the morrow. The old woman had said to summon her if Heather should wake before then.

Madeline sighed. *This is all my fault.* Had she kept her sister with her, she never would have fallen. The girl was stubborn, just like Evelyn, so determined to do things her way. Madeline's heart clenched in her chest. *What if she never wakes?* She shook the question from her mind. Dwelling on the possibilities would lead to undue worry. She turned to dip the cloth in the water basin.

"Maddy," a soft voice croaked. Madeline dropped the cloth and turned with a gasp.

"Heather," she said, tears welling in her eyes. "I am here, my love." She grabbed the child's hand in her own.

"Who won the race?" Heather asked, licking her lips.

Laughter spilled from Madeline. "Lass, you have been injured, and all you can think of is the bloody race." She shook her head. "You are so much like Evelyn it pains me."

"Our cousin?" Heather asked, her eyes bright. Madeline sighed in relief. At least the fall did not damage her mind.

"Aye," she replied softly, squeezing her sister's hand. "Evelyn and I were very close, like sisters."

"I should like to meet her one day." Heather nodded.

Madeline agreed with a nod. "Are you in pain?"

"My arm hurts." Heather winced as she moved it.

"What about your legs?" Madeline asked. "Wiggle your toes, your feet." The blanket twitched with the movement beneath it. Another sigh of relief escaped. She took it as a good sign. Old

Mary had been concerned the fall might have taken her ability to walk. Madeline stood and crossed the room to the door. Opening it, she spotted the guard standing outside.

"Would you be so kind as to fetch Old Mary? Tell her Lady Heather has woken," she said. "Also, tell my father and send up the serving girl." The guard nodded and left her. She returned to Heather's bedside.

"You never answered my question." Heather pouted. "Who won the race?"

"Mackenzie," she replied. "Though it had been close. McLairn and Douglas were right behind him."

"What happened to Alexander?" Heather struggled to sit up.

"Lie down, lass, you will injure yourself further," Madeline admonished. She tucked the girl beneath the blankets again. "Your Alexander is quite well. He found you after your fall and carried you to the keep."

"I fell?" she asked, her face pinkening. "I never fall."

"You should not have been climbing. Ladies do not climb." Madeline saw the shame on her sister's face. "I want you to be safe, my love. You scared us all, especially Alexander. I have never seen him so pale in all my days."

"So he lost the race then because of me?" Heather turned her face away and stared at the wall.

"He carried you to the keep. Not caring one whit whether he finished the race or not," Madeline said, smoothing Heather's hair back from her face.

"He will not win your hand now." Heather's voice echoed with sadness. "And I will be stuck here for the rest of my life."

"Heather." Madeline turned the girl's face until their gazes met. "What are you afraid of? Being left behind?"

"Alexander promised," she said, her voice cracking. "He promised if you married I could come with. He..." Her words broke as the sobs spilled forth.

"There, there, my love." She lay down next to Heather, cradling her head against her bosom. "It will all work out in the end. *Dinnea fash yersel.*" Madeline began to sing softly in Gaelic, a lullaby she vaguely remembered from her childhood. She sang until the door opened and Old Mary popped her silver-haired head in the room.

"She is a strong one," the old woman said as she approached the bed. "Come now, let me see you." While the wise woman examined Heather, Madeline rose and slipped from the room.

She needed some air. Since Heather was safely out of danger, the weight of what had happened came crashing down on top of her. She opened the door to her chamber and stepped inside.

Madeline collapsed on the bed, clutching the pillow to her chest. She had made peace with her father's decision concerning her future, but her heart ached with uncertainty. Not just for herself but for Heather as well. She closed her eyes, knowing she should join the festivities but was not able to bring herself to care.

The great hall was packed full of guests. Laird Campbell stood at the head table. Alexander lingered off to the side of the room, hidden by the shadows near the staircase. Relief washed over him when he heard Heather had woken and there were no injuries save a broken arm. Angus informed him as soon as he heard. Alexander had been standing at the top of the hill overlooking the loch, the sun already gone but still casting streaks of fire red and orange across the sky.

What am I doing here? He scrubbed his hand over his face. He watched the clans mill about the room, their voices mingled in overlapping conversations. A sharp elbow jabbed him in the ribs as Angus joined him.

"Cheer up, all is well," Angus said, handing Alexander a mug of ale. "Aye, you lost the foot race and my sister is injured from failing to emulate a falcon. But look at the positive side..."

"There is a positive side to all of this?" Alexander glanced at him.

"Aye," Angus said, taking a drink. "None of them have killed you yet." He grinned at his own jest.

Alexander rolled his eyes and drank the malted beverage. It left a foul taste in his mouth, both the ale and being here among these strong highland families. *I do not belong here.*

The laird turned toward him and nodded. The moment had arrived. He had been dreading this all day, unsure what reactions would arise from the dour news.

"Attention!" Laird Campbell called out, his deep voice echoing off the stone walls. "I have some news!" Slowly the conversations died down and all attention turned to their host, curious.

"For those of you who are concerned, my daughter is awake. Her injuries are minor, and she will be harassing us all in due course." His words brought a round of cheers through the hall. Truly it was good news, but Alexander knew what was yet to be said and braced himself against the wall.

The laird waved his hands, calming the crowd. When they had sufficiently quieted, he spoke again. "I have also received some bad news from the capitol." A wave of murmurs and chatter shuttled through the guests. He raised his hand again for silence. "Our leader, our king, Robert the Bruce has died."

Shouts and commotion erupted among the guests. The laird yelled over the noise. "There is no cause for alarm. His death came from complications of an illness. The king was suffering, and the Lord saw fit to end his pain." Alexander observed the faces of the men and women in the room: shock, anger, disappointment, fear, uncertainty, pain. He worried these emotions might create an issue.

"Did you know about this?" Angus whispered, leaning closer.

"Aye," he replied. "Your father told me before the race."

Angus stared at him, his jaw hanging. "And you did not think to tell me?" He crossed his arms. "Here I believed we were friends."

"We are," Alexander said, his focus not leaving the

commotion playing out in the great hall.

The laird spoke in an attempt to lull the crowd to the point where he could focus their emotions into something positive. Alexander had seen the baron do the same on several occasions, one of the hallmark traits of being a wise leader, knowing what to say and when to say it. The crowd quieted, their shouts of outrage smoothing into murmurs of begrudging acceptance.

"Our festival will continue as planned. We shall toast to our dear King Robert and celebrate his life and his fight for an independent Scotland." A round of cheers rang throughout the hall. "To King Robert!" he said raising his glass.

"To Robert!" the crowd echoed. They drank in silence.

"Now," Laird Campbell continued. "We feast!" He sat next to his sons, his gaze flickering over Alexander and Angus. The guests indulged in the delicious meal, but Alexander's stomach churned at the thought of food. He wanted to see Heather and talk to Madeline. A smile from her would cure the indecision plaguing his mind.

"Have you seen Madeline?" he asked Angus.

Angus shook his head. "Nay. I shall check to see if she is still with Heather." He stole up the stairs. Alexander wanted to follow him, but he knew such an action on his part would be inappropriate. So he stood in the corner, silently watching and wishing the situation would have been different.

Chapter Eleven

Madeline smoothed the green gown down over her hips. She tied the green and blue kirtle, pinning a silver brooch over her heart. Tucking a stray hair into place, she took a settling breath. Her unseemly absence did nothing to alter the fact she was the reason everyone attended the tournament. Isolating herself was a selfish, childish way for a lady to behave. Indeed, was it not her job to play hostess? She reached for the handle when a knock startled her. Pressing her hand to her chest, Madeline opened the door.

"We were growing concerned at your absence," Angus said, wearing an easy smile. "Care to join the feast?" He offered his arm to her. She kissed his cheek, touched by his concern.

"I want to check on Heather then I shall be down directly," she promised. He nodded and walked down the corridor.

She pushed open Heather's door. The fire in the hearth cast shadows across the room. Madeline worried at her sister's injury. The girl's penchant for climbing had caused this. She held her candle close, peeking at her sister as she slept. Deep in sleep, Heather appeared peaceful. Madeline sighed in relief. If only she had kept Heather close during the race, this never would have happened. No use worrying over something which she had no control. With one last glance, she left the room. Closing the door quietly, she turned and ran into a solid wall of highland muscle.

"You startled me," she said, breathless, half expecting Alexander. Madeline raised the candle, and the dark eyes of Willem Douglas stared back at her.

"I beg your pardon," he said, his brogue rough and his breath tainted with the strong odor of ale. "I was hoping to steal a moment alone with you." He leaned closer, backing her against the wall, his hands on the stone. *Trapped.* Her heart raced. He was a handsome devil but notorious for his temper, especially when he had been drinking.

"Would you let me pass?" She pushed at his arm. But he was fixed, unmoving and his gaze burned into her, making her extremely uncomfortable. "I beg you, let me pass."

"For a price," he murmured. "A kiss for your freedom." His eyes glinted, dark and haunting in the candlelight.

"A kiss?" Madeline glanced to the left and saw nothing but an empty corridor. Panic crept into her mind.

She pressed her hand against his chest in an attempt to push him back. "You have drunk too much ale." Madeline turned her face from him as he leaned closer. His breath on her cheek and the press of his body against hers made her head ache. She could scream but to what end. All he wanted was a kiss, one harmless kiss. "If I grant you a kiss, will you please let me go?"

Douglas watched her from beneath hooded lids. "On my honor as a Douglas," he replied, his voice low. She turned to face him, their lips a breath apart. She leaned forward, pressing her lips to the corner of his mouth in a chaste kiss. His hand grasped the back of her head, fingers slipping into her hair, as he slanted his lips to meet hers. The contact surprised her, unexpected but not unpleasant. The kiss ended before she could protest. As he pulled back, his eyes shone like the color of midnight, his breathing rapid.

He dropped his hands and stepped away, allowing her to leave at her leisure.

"What in the bloody hell is going on here?" Madeline's head spun toward the sound of Alexander's voice. He took a step closer, his expression thunderous. "Did he force himself on you, my lady?"

Madeline glanced between the men. Their stares locked. She could almost feel the tension rising between them like a serpent from the grass. Her heart pounded as she saw the two men glare at each other. Guilt and shame washed over her. What would Alexander do? She could not bear the idea of them coming to blows over her mistake.

"Alexander, I am well," she said, glancing at Douglas. "Willem was just..." She hesitated to lie, for she assumed he had seen their embrace.

"He was kissing you." Alexander finished her thought, not even looking at her. "What right do you have to kiss her?"

"As much right as you have, *Sassenach*," Douglas replied without flinching.

Madeline stepped between them. "Willem, I beg of you, stop such talk." Her heart jumped into her throat. *How did Douglas know Alexander was English?* Her stomach lurched wondering what would happen to Alexander if the rest of the clans knew the truth.

Alexander glared at Douglas but did not speak.

"A lowlander," Douglas spat. "He might as well be English."

Madeline breathed a sigh of relief. At least Alexander's secret remained safe. "Willem..." Before she could finish, Alexander lunged for Douglas, shoving Madeline out of the way. She stumbled and fell against the wall. Madeline scrambled to her feet, turning to see Alexander and Douglas grappling on the floor. The crack of fist against flesh and bone made her shudder.

"Stop this madness!" she screamed, but they paid her no heed. She would be useless trying to pull them apart. Madeline dashed down the hall and met her brothers on the stairs.

"Help me," she shouted and raced back down the hall. Angus grabbed hold of Douglas while Rodric dragged Alexander back, pinning his arms behind him. The two men struggled like wild animals. *All this over me?*

"Both of you should be ashamed of yourselves." She glared at both of them in turn. "I do not belong to anyone yet. Until such a time as I am wed, I will kiss whomever I bloody well choose!"

Alexander had a cut above his eye, the blood running down his cheek, while Douglas sported a darkening ring along his left cheek. She did not even care anymore. Madeline turned on her heel, stomped down the stairs, and walked straight out the door. The night air immediately refreshed her, and the tension faded into the background.

Madeline walked out the postern gate and up the hill. *Idiotic men, stupid, bloody, thoughtless*...the curses streamed in her head threatening to bubble from her lips. She muttered under her breath, allowing the soft curses to vent to the night. She kicked a stone, and it disappeared into the tall grass.

The view of the loch from the top of the hill immediately calmed her. She used stand atop the hill as a child, staring out into the vast landscape and hoping. *Hoping for what?* Her dreams withered daily with the impending announcement of her marriage.

Her musings wandered to Evelyn. Madeline wrapped her arms around herself. Was her cousin happy? Moments like those made Madeline miss her friend. They shared everything. Their hopes and dreams. Their most secret desires. Now she was alone, having driven off the one man she truly loved.

She cursed. *Why did I kiss Douglas? Why did I acquiesce to his demand?* He could be handsome and charming when he wanted to be. Alexander had seen everything. She hung her head, mortified. Douglas surprised her though, by not taking advantage of her as she believed he would.

"Och, what a bloody mess," she whispered to the highland hills.

"Such foul language from such a beautiful lady." Madeline turned to see McLairn standing a few paces behind her.

"I beg your pardon," she said, covering her mouth. "I believed I was alone."

"What are you doing out here alone, by the by?" he asked, joining her.

She sighed. "I needed to think. The evening's events have upset me more than I realized."

He nodded. "'Tis a tragedy to lose our king so soon."

"What?" she asked, surprised and saddened by his words.

"The announcement your father made at the feast." He studied her reaction. "King Robert has died. I assumed it was the reason for your unhappiness." McLairn furrowed his brow. "Does something else have you troubled?"

"Nay," she replied, heaving a heavy sigh. *How many things could go wrong in one day?* Surely he heard of the fight. Madeline chose not to tell him about it. The tournament embarrassed her enough, having men compete for her hand, let alone two of them coming to blows for her favor. She feared what would happen if one challenged the other. Their last play with swords had ended on a sour note.

"Your father is concerned about you." His voice sounded like the touch of satin, so smooth it wrapped around her like a blanket.

"He always is."

"I am concerned as well," he said, taking her hand in his. The moonlight illuminated his face, his sharp features softened by the glow. All of her suitors were handsome and strong, but she felt nothing for them. *Except Alexander.*

"You are?" she parroted, unsure where the conversation was leading.

"Aye." McLairn smoothed his fingers across the back of her knuckles. The touch made her shiver. *If he tries to kiss me...*she let the concern slowly melt into her subconscious. Alexander could not save her this time. She exhaled, unaware she had been holding her breath.

"I am perfectly well, as you can see," she said, a nervous smile on her lips.

"I am not blind, my lady." His brogue thickened with every word. "You have your heart set on Alexander." She tried not to react, to keep her expression impassive. "'Tis written on your face when I mention his name."

She cursed her poor ability to hide her emotions. McLairn gripped her hand between his own, the pressure pinching her skin. Madeline flinched.

"I have no idea what you are talking about," she snapped. "Release me." *What possesses these men and encourages their domineering ways?* She should have stayed in the keep, stayed with Heather. She was in no mood to deal with these highlanders.

He pulled her against him. "You are hiding something, lass. I can always tell when someone is lying. Call it a gift."

Madeline struggled against him, trying to break from his grip. "I said release me!" she screamed, jerking and twisting. *'Tis hopeless.* He stood a head taller, his grip tightening around her arms, making her wince in pain. She collapsed against him, tired of fighting, tired of it all.

"She gave you a bloody order." Alexander grabbed McLairn by the arm and wrenched it back, bending it at an unnatural angle. McLairn cried out and released Madeline from his grip. She dashed away from him, rubbing her hand.

"Get your sorry arse out of here." He pushed McLairn away in disgust.

The highlander stumbled back, clutching his arm to his chest. "You will regret that, lowlander," he murmured, the threat unmistakable.

Madeline cringed, afraid he might actually do something to hurt Alexander. She held her breath as he turned and left them. A shiver wracked her. Twice in one night she had been accosted by men who wanted to take her to wife. *Like bloody hell.* Alexander laid his hand on her shoulder.

"Did he harm you?" he asked, concern etched on his brow.

"Nay." She shook her head. "He…Alexander, you must go. Return to the baron. Get as far away from here as you can." Madeline backed up, her heart aching at the truth as it came pouring from her lips. "When they find out," she whispered, letting the implication trail off.

"Madeline." The way her name rolled off his tongue broke her heart.

"Nay, you need to leave before they discover the truth. You cannot hide it forever. And what if you do win my hand?" She hung her head. "It can never be."

Alexander stood there, his arms stiffly at his sides, his demeanor as cold as ice. "If it is what you wish."

Madeline pushed past him to return to the keep, unable to reply. The tears pooled in her eyes. She dashed them away with the back of her hand. He did not need to see her cry. Did not need to see how much it pained her to let him go. He would be safe, and her father would be happy with her decision. When she reached the bottom of the hill, she slipped into the postern gate. She did not need to turn around to know he followed her.

"Alexander." Angus approached from the far side of the

bailey. He glanced at Madeline as she ran past him, desperate to be alone in her chambers. She barely heard her brother call after her as the door slammed behind her.

Angus glanced at Alexander. "Did you hurt her?" he asked, crossing his arms.

Alexander stared at him. If the man believed he would hurt the one woman he valued more than life itself, then he was blind as well as stupid.

"My father would like to have a word with you," Angus said, dropping the subject. "Alone. In his presence chambers. Now."

Alexander raised a brow in question. It seemed most likely his fight with Douglas and McLairn had reached the laird's attention. He was supposed to be befriending the clansmen, not making enemies.

"Aye," he replied, heading for the great hall. When he reached the door to the chamber, Alexander resigned himself to his fate and knocked.

"Enter."

Alexander opened the door and saw Laird Campbell sitting in front of the fire, a glass of whisky in his hand. He motioned for Alexander to join him.

As Alexander sank into the chair, his gaze rested on the man who held more power over him than he would have liked. He waited for the laird to speak.

"You have caused quite a commotion," he said after a few tense moments. "It has come to my attention you have quite a talent for burrowing beneath the wrong skin."

"I am not sure I follow," Alexander said slowly.

"First, you start a brawl with Willem Douglas. Then I receive a complaint from Thomas McLairn about your behavior in front of my daughter." He took a drink. "What am I to make of this? I thought we were of an accord."

"We are, my laird." Alexander shifted in his seat.

"But you are no closer to discovering who has been stealing from me?"

"Nay." The conversation's direction did not bode well for him. Alexander stared into the fire, unable to meet the old man's gaze.

"These are dangerous times."

Alexander studied him. "Aye, they are."

The laird set his glass down on the table beside him. He leaned forward, his sharp gaze making Alexander uncomfortable.

"You have proven yourself, time and again, to be an honorable man, Sir Alexander. It would be unwise for me to overlook your selfless acts, and your selfish ones as well." He put his hand up. "Angus told me what happened with Douglas. I do not care what happened with McLairn."

"McLairn..." Alexander began, determined the laird should know what kind of men competed for his daughter's hand.

"McLairn will not be marrying my daughter," the laird said, leaning back in his chair.

Alexander sat, stunned. *Has he already chosen the winner?* He wanted to ask, the words itching the tip of his tongue. But he kept his mouth closed, waiting.

"I am naming you the winner of the tournament," he said, a grin tugging on the corners of his mouth.

"Me?" Alexander felt the words choking him, but he sputtered until they came out. "My laird, I did not win..."

"You won my trust, Sir Alexander, and the love of my daughter. Each game embodied more than a merely tests of strength and skill. They were a test of honor. To see what kind of mettle you were made of." The laird stood.

Alexander stared at him, dumbstruck. As much as he wanted Madeline, he feared she would not have him now. She had a point. He was English, at least partially, and his allegiance, his fealty oath, lay with an English lord. Perhaps a union between them would not be wise.

"But what of the truth?" Alexander asked as he stood. "When they find out I am English, there will be problems which arise because of your decision."

"We shall not tell them." He winked. "Not yet at least. They need not discover the truth until you are wed and safely returned to the baron."

"They will surely..." Alexander began, but the laird cut him off.

"'Tis my concern, lad. Your concern now is taking care of my daughter." He clapped a hand on Alexander's shoulder.

Alexander nodded, still reeling from the news when he remembered a promise he made to a young girl.

"My laird," Alexander began, unsure how he would react. "I would like to take Heather with us when we return."

Laird Campbell stroked his beard in thought. "The lass is a wild thing. It would be good for her to stay with her sister for a bit, finally learn to be a proper lady." He nodded in agreement. "Aye, she may go. But do not tell her where you are going. The girl cannot keep a secret to save her life."

Alexander shook his hand. "I will do my best to keep them safe, my laird." He turned to go.

"Alexander," the laird said, and he paused. "Send Angus in."

Chapter Twelve

Madeline pulled the hood up over her head and leaned over to blow out the candle. She slipped out of her chamber and down the corridor. The keep stood shrouded in darkness, except for the fire burning in the hearth of the great hall. She had left a note for her father. Surely, he would not worry overmuch. As Madeline stepped out into the moonlight, she made her way to the stables. The postern gate remained open allowing the guests to come and go freely from the keep.

After quickly saddling her horse, she grabbed the reins and swung herself onto the mare's back. Madeline gave a soft click to urge her forward. They slipped from the keep and out onto the moors leading down toward the loch. Her father kept a hunting lodge on the far side of An Loch Meadhanach. The moon lit the path as they moved quietly. She glanced over her shoulder at the receding keep. No one would miss her until the morning, and by then she would be tucked safely away at the lodge.

Madeline had enough of their games, the politics and the assaults on her person. She refused to be a prize sow for them to manhandle and caress upon their leisure. A pang of regret settled in her chest. She had promised her father she would do her duty to the family. But the events of the day weighed heavily on her, to the point where she could not even take a breath without physical pain overwhelming her.

A well-worn path wove into the trees. Moonlight spotted through the leaves, creating a dappled gray pattern on the dirt. She pushed forward with the knowledge of peace awaiting her at the lodge.

The snap of a twig behind her jerked her from the reverie. She twisted in the saddle, searching the trees, when she saw him in the shadows.

"Who goes there? Show yourself." She mustered her

courage and spun the horse around to face him. Her hand rested on the dagger strapped to her hip. Madeline knew to stick them with the pointy end, and that was all the instruction that mattered to her. "Answer me."

The shadows separated, and a man in black materialized. His head covered with an archer's hood, his face hidden deep in its recesses.

"You," she sputtered, her breath catching in her chest. *The man from the garden, the one who kissed me.* "What are you doing here?"

"I am here to protect you, my lady," he said, his voice low. "Why do you stray from the safety of your family?"

"I must take some time to think," she replied, the honesty of her words surprising her. *Why am I telling a stranger this? Nay, not a stranger.* She had dreamt of him for weeks. The memory of his stolen kiss haunted her. She tilted her head, watching him. "Who are you?"

"I am a Shadow Guardian." He reached out with a gloved hand and stroked her horse's muzzle. "'Tis my duty to protect you, even from yourself."

"I do not need your protection." Madeline sniffed, as he stepped closer. His hand glided across the horse's sleek neck and came to rest next to her leg. She bit her lip. Would he return her to the keep by force? She backed the horse up, but he snatched the reins from her hand.

"What do you want from me?" Panic and desire fluttered in her chest. She wanted him to kiss her again. The realization shocked her, even as the truth of the words flooded her body with warmth she had not anticipated. Something familiar and comforting about him called to her. A small hint of recognition fluttered in the back of her mind. One more kiss and she could be sure her mind was not merely playing tricks on her.

His hand came to rest on her thigh and slid up to her waist. He pulled her down from the saddle and into his arms.

"I want you." He dipped his head to kiss her. The tenderness of his kiss made her melt against him, and Madeline knew. She gripped his cloak, pulling him closer, wanting more contact. His lips parted over hers, and she sighed when he tasted her. Suddenly the dam burst, and she poured her heart into the kiss, her body arching against his.

"Madeline," he whispered against her lips. Her brain fogged by the heat surging through her, and she nodded, unable to reply.

"I have to tell you..." His breath brushed over her wet lips.

She wanted him to shut up and kiss her again, to forget the tournament and the promises, her duty and responsibilities. This moment belonged to them, and she savored it. But he persisted.

"Look at me," he said, tilting her chin up. She opened her eyes and stared into the darkened shadows of his face.

"Alexander," she whispered, reaching up and pulling the hood back. The moonlight hit his face just right, revealing the sharp features she had come to adore. So her mind and her heart were in accord. She had known, deep in her soul.

"How?" His brow furrowed in confusion.

"When you kissed me in the garden, then again in my chamber," she explained. "Just like in this very moment, your kiss sets my heart racing, my stomach aflutter. The touch of your skin to mine is like magic. I would know you anywhere."

A grin broke across his lips. She kissed him again, the passion building as she tangled her fingers in his hair. He moaned as her teeth grazed his lower lip, drawing it into her mouth.

"Where did you learn to do such things?" he asked when she released him.

Madeline shrugged. "Is that a complaint?" Her tongue darted across her lips, forcing his gaze to settle on her mouth.

"Nay." He sighed, as their lips met again.

A distant rumble of thunder echoed through the valley. He pulled away. "We should return before the storm comes."

"I have a better idea," she said, picking up her horse's reins. "Do you have a horse?" Alexander nodded. "Go fetch him."

He helped her back onto her mount and fetched his own. Side by side, they ambled through the trees until Madeline spotted a break in the forest, which looked familiar, even by moonlight.

""Tis just around this bend." She led him into the thickening forest, winding down a narrow path to a hillside made of stone. A yawning mouth opened along the rocky ledge, the darkness inviting them to come inside the cave.

They dismounted, and Alexander tied their horses to the branches of a nearby tree just as the first raindrops began to fall. Madeline glanced at the sky. The moon peeked from behind a cloud as the rain came down harder and faster.

"Come," she called as she snatched up pieces of wood lying near the cave entrance. Alexander gathered some as well. A flash of lightning lit the sky, a crash of thunder echoing behind it. The horses reared and pulled free of their ties. They bolted, heading back the way they had come. He turned and followed Madeline into the cave.

"How did you know of this place?" he said, pulling a flint from his pocket. She arranged a small pile of sticks on the ground.

"My brothers used to hide here when we were children," she said. "I followed them once. They used to bring girls here all the time." Madeline remembered her oldest brother kissing the milkmaid here. She had been hiding behind the rock outside. He pushed the girl against the rock and kissed her, just like Alexander had done to her. Madeline's cheeks heated at the memory.

The fire ignited, a tiny flame bursting from the dry branches and kindling. Madeline helped Alexander build the fire up until a comfortable warmth emanated from it. She sat down on the dirt, brushing her hair back over her shoulder. The silence stretched between them. The crackling of the fire and the rain created a melodic cadence.

"Why do you wear such garb?" Madeline said, unable to take the silence a moment longer.

"What garb?" Alexander sat down next to her, brushing his hands off on his trousers.

"All black, the hood, sneaking around and scaring the life out of people." She loved how the firelight played off his handsome features. In the last few days, she had learned more about him than she ever believed possible. Still the question haunted her. "What is a Shadow Guardian?"

Alexander exhaled. "It was my father's idea." He glanced at her. "My father hated the idea of a tear between our nations because of the tension between England and Scotland. He trained us to be protectors, to maintain the peace on the border and create a safe place for families on both sides who were unfortunately caught in the middle of a political struggle."

"Us?" she asked, intrigued by his tale. Her admiration for Alexander blossomed as he spoke. He never spoke of himself, so she indulged in his story as a drunkard would summer wine.

"My brothers and me," he replied, turning toward her. "Now you understand why my place is with the baron. It is my duty to ensure there is peace on the border. The day your brother came to fetch you, an attempt had been made on the baron's life. Richard had plotted to kill him and marry Evelyn to ensure his power over the barony."

Madeline pressed her hand to her chest. She had not realized any of this. Never even thought to ask. "Why did you not tell me?"

"You were dealing with problems of your own," he said softly. "I did not want to overburden you. There was naught you could do."

"Did they arrest Richard?" she asked.

"Nay." He frowned. "He escaped in the commotion during the tournament. It was not until the next day we even realized you had gone missing." Alexander met her gaze, regret apparent in his expression. "I left as soon as I could."

"You should not have concerned yourself about me," she said. "As you can see, I am well."

"Madeline," he whispered as he slid his hand into hers. "I meant what I said that night in the garden. I have wanted you from the moment I saw you."

Her breath hitched as he drew her into his lap. She nestled against his chest and leaned her head on his shoulder, the warmth from the fire matched by the warmth of his body. Her hand tangled in his hair, and she curled it around her finger. His hand splayed across her hip, holding her close. She felt safe and warm in his arms. Her eyes drifted closed.

"I did as well," she whispered the confession against his neck. "You stole my breath away, even with your stern expression." Madeline traced his jaw with a fingertip. "I prayed you would notice me."

He exhaled sharply. "I did, Lord knows I did. Every time you walked into a room, every time you smiled, I noticed." He tipped her chin up. "I was a fool for not confessing my admiration."

Madeline beamed at him. "Such a handsome fool," she said as she leaned in to kiss him.

His groan rumbled through her. She twisted in his arms and straddled his thighs, hoping to get better access to his lips. His hands slid beneath her cloak, pulling her against him.

"I wanted to beg your forgiveness," she whispered, ignoring the delicious friction building between them. His every breath brushed against her cheek like a stolen caress. Madeline tried to focus on the apology, but being so close to him muddled her mind.

"For what?" His fingertips danced on her spine. She bit her lip, pushing away the distraction of his touch. His gaze settled on her lips. The shadows sharpened every curve of his face. Her heart fluttered.

"I...well...for kissing Douglas," she stammered, embarrassed to even bring it up. Alexander's gaze narrowed a bit, and he cocked his head. His hands never stilled. They tortured her with their subtle exploration.

"Hmmm..." He murmured. "Did you enjoy it?"

"Nay!" She held his gaze. "He cornered me and told me he would release me in exchange for a kiss."

"Did he now?" Alexander seemed far from pleased about the direction of the conversation.

"He did...let me go once I kissed him," she said in a rush, the words jumbling together.

"Aye." Alexander stilled, his hands resting lightly on her hips. "I know."

"You saw?" Madeline cocked her head, confused. "But if

you saw him let me go, then why did you hit him? You could have just challenged him. Or informed my father."

"I could have." He nodded. "But he deserved to have his arse beaten."

Madeline stared at him. She had been raised with brothers, but she would never understand the way a man's mind worked.

"Besides," Alexander continued. "He kissed the woman I love."

Those words caught her attention. "Wait, what did you just say?" Madeline held her breath, her mind spinning.

"I love you, Madeline," he said. "More than life itself. I always have."

She felt the tears gathering and wiped them with the sleeve of her gown.

"Why are you crying, love?" His concern touched her soul, and she laughed at the silliness of her tears. None of it mattered though.

"My father, the tournament," she stammered, a sob threatening to choke her. "I have an obligation to my family. My father has yet to choose a husband for me."

Alexander stared at her, conspicuously silent. The sob broke through, followed by the tears. He said nothing but pulled her against him, urging her to lay her head against his chest with his hand.

This would be her only moment of peace with him. Tomorrow he would escort her to the keep and into the hands of the man her father chose. A sliver of her heart cried out. *Pick Alexander, please. Pick him.* Father would be angry at being misled, to know an English knight competed for the hand of his daughter. She clutched Alexander's shirt, burying her face against him, hiding her shame, her tears. She tried to tell him to leave, tried to do the right thing. But she would be forever ruined for another man. Her heart belonged to Alexander.

They sat in silence. He stroked her hair, the soft motion lulling her to sleep. She closed her eyes, listening to the sound of his heartbeat and the crackle and pop of the fire.

"I wish you were mine," she murmured before falling asleep

in his embrace.

Chapter Thirteen

Angus rode down the trail leading back to the keep from the hunting lodge. The day had barely started when a servant had barreled into his chamber shouting a summons from his father. That had been several hours ago. Tired and agitated, he craved nothing but the comfort of his bed.

"Madeline, you daft lass, where in the bloody hell are you?" he muttered to the trees as he rode. The servant had found a note on Madeline's bed saying she had gone to the lodge for some time to think. She must have left right before the storm came in. The paths were thick with mud and the air smelled fresher, cleaner.

Two horses had returned to the keep, riderless. His father feared foul play might be involved. Angus volunteered to check the hunting lodge while the other brothers scoured the village and the countryside. He rode directly to the lodge, found nothing and left completely puzzled. He had been unable to track a thing since the rain had washed any tracks away. With a sigh, he pulled his horse to a stop.

Perhaps the storm caught her unaware and she sought out shelter. He glanced around. Nothing along the trail offered shelter...then he remembered. The cave they used to play in as children. He reined his horse to follow the small deer path leading to the cave. Reaching the mouth, he dismounted and peeked into the darkened opening. The sunlight shone through the trees, shedding just enough light for Angus to make out two figures lying in the dirt, their limbs intertwined.

Angus could not help but grin. He had gone to fetch Alexander to come with him but found his tent empty. It figured he had gone with her, or after her, or kidnapped her. It really did not matter one whit to him what Alexander did. He enjoyed the man's company and approved of his character. English or Scot, blood be damned. He had not been the only one who noticed their absence. This could cause problems for the laird should the truth be discovered.

Angus stepped into the cave and kicked Alexander's booted foot.

"Get your lazy arses up!" he shouted. In a flurry of movement, Alexander released Madeline and jumped to his feet, his dagger drawn. When he spotted Angus, he swore and sheathed the blade. Madeline struggled to get to her feet. Alexander offered his hand for her to steady herself. She turned on Angus, her hair a wild mess, her brow furrowed, and lips pursed.

"How dare you!" She swung at him, her fist colliding with his arm. His sister might be petite, but she had a lot of anger balled up in her fist. He rubbed the spot and chuckled.

"How dare I?" he sputtered. "Father has the whole of the highlands out searching for you right now." He looked pointedly at Alexander. "And what is your role in all of this?"

"I followed her," Alexander replied, his face impassive. "She slipped out on horseback. I followed behind until the storm hit. We found shelter with the intention of waiting it out then returning to the keep."

"Is that all that happened?" Angus had to fight to keep a smirk from breaking the serious expression on his face. He wanted to laugh at them. The love they had for each other was written on their faces, certainly, but they were not lovers. Not yet at least.

Madeline glanced at Alexander, then back to Angus. "Nothing happened, you gormless clod!" She stormed from the cave, brushing past him close enough to jab her elbow in his ribs. He lurched at the pain shooting through his side and cast her an injured look. She tossed her head and disappeared from view.

Angus let out a low whistle. "What did you do to her to put her in such a foul mood?"

Alexander stared at him. "Who said it was I who put her in a foul mood?"

"Women," Angus muttered under his breath. "I did naught to deserve such a greeting."

Alexander gathered his things and walked toward the sunlight. Angus grabbed his arm. "My father is upset—" he met Alexander's gaze "—and he is not the only one."

The knight paused. "What do you mean?"

"When my father sent us to search for Madeline, word spread quickly you had absconded with my sister." He paused. "The clans believe you claimed her before you had a right to, and they demand justice."

Alexander rubbed his hand across his face. "What has your father said?"

"He has not said a word to anyone; neither confirming nor denying the rumor." Angus had hoped to find them before the others. Alexander was not the scoundrel they believed him to be. No one knew the truth of the laird's true plan, not even Madeline.

"We should return then and address the misunderstanding," Alexander said. "If we explained what happened, then your father will understand."

"My father is not the one I worry about understanding. McLairn has already called for you to be disqualified from the tournament."

"I am sure we can come to an agreement," Alexander mused, but Angus could see the concern in his expression.

"If word gets out you spent the night together, alone..." Angus trailed off with a shrug. "They will assume the worst."

"They would think I did it on purpose to claim Madeline as my own." Alexander's voice sounded strained. He straightened and turned to Angus. "I thank you for the warning. We should return before they grow restless."

Angus nodded and followed Alexander from the cave.

Madeline waited astride Angus' horse. She did not speak but gave the horse a nudge into motion.

"Looks like we are walking," Angus said, slapping Alexander on the back. It would be a long day. He just hoped it ended well. He knew all too well when a man felt slighted, he often made stupid decisions.

Madeline rode ahead of the men, refusing to speak to them. Her mind raced, and she pressed her lips together to keep from speaking out of anger. As if Angus had the authority to tell her what to do. She was tired of it all, the tournament, the charade, all of it. When she returned to the keep, she would tell her father exactly what she thought of this whole arrangement. He could take her promise and cast it into the loch with the fish.

The horse trudged through the mud as they came into the clearing. Madeline could see the stone walls of the keep reaching for the sky. Glancing over her shoulder, she spied the two men walking side by side. Their legs covered in mud. They stomped and kicked, trying to shake it off or wipe it in the tall grass. She stifled a giggle. *They deserve it.* She nudged the horse into a trot, leaving Alexander and Angus behind.

As soon as she reached the postern gate, she slowed the horse to a walk and entered the keep. Her father stood in the bailey, giving instructions to the stable boy. He turned and caught sight of her. She swallowed. *Now or never.*

"Madeline," he said, his voice stern but laced with concern. "We were worried for you, lass. Why in the blazes would you run off in the middle of the night? You could have been injured, or worse." He helped her down off the horse and handed the reins to the stable boy.

"Father, I am well. No harm has come to me." Madeline embraced him, and then took his arm as he led her toward the great hall.

"You must be famished," he said, patting her arm. "Come, Cook will find something for you in the kitchens." He wanted to speak again but pursed his lips together in hesitation.

"Say it." Madeline knew the look spoke of a forthcoming lecture. She could feel it in her bones. He reached up and stroked his beard. *Och, not now.* It was a tell-tale sign he pondered a difficult decision.

He turned to Madeline, taking her face between his callused

hands. "Lass, you look like your mother, rest her soul. You have her sweet spirit as well." He sighed. "I would hate to see you broken at the hands of a man who would not care for you properly. I have a confession to make."

Madeline's blood froze. *What is he talking about?* She blinked, a bit confused by his statement, but her frustration soon overwhelmed it. "What confession, Father?"

He glanced around the empty bailey, making sure no one lingered to hear his words. He shook his head. "Come with me, child. I will tell you."

Her father led her into the great hall, sent a servant to fetch her some food, and hurried into his presence chamber. Madeline sat in the chair by the hearth as he closed the door.

"The tournament, the festivities, are all for show, Madeline. I never had any intention of marrying you to any of them." He sat down in the chair across from her.

Madeline felt as though a horse had kicked her square in the chest. "What?" she whispered, her blood thundering in her head. Perhaps the lack of food made her faint, but her body swayed with the news. "Why did you bring me here then?" Her voice sounded sharper than she had intended, anger tainting her words.

"'Tis a long story," he said, leaning back in his chair.

"We have the time," she replied. "I am listening."

He sighed. "Your brothers have noticed cattle missing from the herds. They have also noticed some of the smaller villages are being frequented by thieves. My people expect me to take care of them in all things. I could not protect them without knowing who was causing all the trouble."

Madeline sat back and crossed her arms, listening to his tale. She understood the responsibilities of the laird were much like the ones her uncle dealt with in his barony.

Her father continued, "I made the announcement of the tournament and sent invitations to all the clans surrounding our lands. One of them had to be behind the thefts. I needed a prize worth the risk." He met her gaze. "I needed you to lure them here, lass."

Madeline felt as though she had been struck. "You used me as bait?" Her heart pounded in her chest as her hands clenched in rage. Her eyes burned with tears. She blinked them away.

"Aye, *m'eudail.*" *My dear.* He leaned forward and laid his hand on her knee. "There was no other way."

"Och, you should have told me," she said, her brogue returning. The bitterness dripped from each word. "I deserved to know."

Her father nodded. "Forgive me for deceiving you." His gaze filled with concern as he held his hand out. She reluctantly placed her palm against his. He squeezed her hand. "I am sending you back to the baron and your cousin."

"Back?" she murmured, confused by his decision.

"Aye." His thumb smoothed across the back of her hand. "The clans are upset. They believe you eloped with Alexander. None of them saw you return, so I will send you on your way this evening."

Madeline's head spun. "What about Heather? I cannot just leave her here. Let me take her with me, I beg you." She clutched his hand between her own, willing him to grant her this one request.

The laird heaved a heavy sigh. "If she is able to travel, you may take her with you. She needs to learn her place. Climbing trees and threatening servants with a dagger is not ladylike behavior." He dropped her hand and stood, pacing in front of the fire. "Did you return of your own volition?"

His question startled her. She had forgotten about Angus and Alexander. They would have made it to the keep by now. She glanced at the fire, the heat from her memories fanning the blush rising in her cheeks.

"Angus found me this morning," she replied, purposefully leaving out the details of Alexander and how she spent the night in his arms. Madeline pressed a cool hand to her face.

"So you were at the lodge when he found you?"

"Nay, I was caught in the storm. My horse bolted, and I spent the night in the cave down by the loch."

"Alone?" the laird asked, his sharp gaze on her.

"Aye."

"Two horses returned in the night. Riderless." He stroked his beard. "Did you ride both of them?"

Madeline swore under her breath. Her father arched a brow at her.

"Alexander saw me leave during the night," she said. "He followed, confronting me down by the loch. We could not make it back to the keep before the storm fell upon us, so we sought shelter in the cave for the night. The horses were spooked by the thunder." Madeline chewed her lower lip. "Nothing happened, father. He behaved with chivalry."

The laird nodded, obviously lost in thought. He turned to her again. "Did Angus find you both in the cave?"

"Aye." Madeline buried her face in her hands, sighed, and faced her father again. "I took Angus' horse and made both of them walk."

His bark of laughter startled her, and he leaned against the hearth mantle. "You are your mother's daughter, lass."

Her lips twitched into a grin at the mention of her mother. But inside, her heart raced and her mind reeled with questions.

"You will not hurt him, will you, Father?" She twisted her hands in her skirt.

"*Dinnea fash yersel,*" he said as he pulled her to her feet. "Go to your chambers. I shall call for a meal and a bath for you. Then rest yourself. Sleeping on the cold hard cave floor must have been uncomfortable."

Madeline felt the heat rising in her cheeks again. She pushed the memory of Alexander's strong arms around her from her mind. She turned to her father, wrapping him in a hug before opening the door and running into two mud-covered, infuriated, and sweaty Scots.

Alexander and Angus stood in her way. With a delicate sniff, she pushed past them, heading for her chambers. She heard her father shout for a servant and felt them watching her as she retreated to the seclusion of her chamber.

Chapter Fourteen

Alexander stood mesmerized by the sway of her hips as she walked away. He suppressed a groan. The prior night had been one of the most difficult of his life. He had been content just to hold her, but when she murmured in her sleep, her body arched against his. He shoved the memory away with two hands, burying it in the back of his mind.

"Come in."

Angus led, followed by Alexander.

The old man poured three glasses of Scotch. Picking up two, he handed them to the mud-covered younger men. Alexander guarded his tongue, unsure what Madeline had told her father. He sipped the strong liquor as he waited for Laird Campbell to speak.

"Sit down, lads," he said, his tone betraying nothing.

Alexander grimaced as he sat. His back ached from lying in such an awkward position during the night. He caught Angus' grin out of the corner of his eye. For a moment, he almost mistook Angus for Gabriel, with the stupid smirk and laughing eyes.

"The cave makes a handy shelter but a very poor bed." The laird stroked his beard as he eyed Alexander.

"Aye." Alexander did not know what to say, so he kept his replies as simple as possible.

"Did you make my daughter aware of our understanding?"

Alexander remembered his conversation with Madeline the night before. As well as the smoldering kisses they shared and the way she fit so perfectly nestled against him. He shook his head.

"Nay." He had wanted to tell her, but something made him hold back. *Fear?* He had no idea. At this moment though, he had courage in liquid form. Taking a fortifying drink, he met the laird's inquisitive gaze.

"I will need you to take on a task for me, Alexander."

"Aye, anything you ask. I am at your service." Alexander downed the rest of the amber liquid.

"I need you to listen carefully, for your life may very well depend on this." The laird sat across from him and sipped his drink. "Angus informed you of the frustrations brewing among our guests, did he not?"

"Aye, he said they believe I claimed Madeline before a winner could be declared," Alexander replied.

Angus brought over the decanter and poured more whisky in his cup.

"They believe this had been your intent all along, but I informed them you were aiding Angus in the search for Madeline, not the cause of her disappearance." The laird watched him as he absorbed the information. "Not everyone believes my tale, however."

"Douglas and McLairn?"

"Aye." The elder Campbell nodded and then finished his whisky. "They have been on your scent since the first night you arrived. It does not help you have picked a fight with both of them before Madeline disappeared. To them, you are guilty."

Alexander sighed. "What would you have me do?"

"I need you to aid Angus in escorting Madeline and Heather safely to the Baron of Rayne." He leaned forward, resting his elbows on his knees. "I have drawn up the necessary letters for the baron, and you shall be ready to ride this eve after the sun sets."

Alexander glanced at Angus, then back to Laird Campbell. "Aye, my laird, as you wish."

The laird nodded as he stroked his beard. "Last eve I told you of my intention to name you the winner of the tournament. I offered you Madeline's hand in marriage. The offer remains on the table, should you choose to take it."

"Have you informed Madeline of this offer?" Alexander clenched his fist around the cup, wondering when the ax would swing and shatter the moment.

Laird Campbell shook his head. "I informed her of the

reason for the tournament, and that she is free of any obligation to marry the winner."

"But would that not mean your prior statement is now nullified?" Alexander caught the bemused expression on Angus' face out of the corner of his eye and chose to ignore it.

"Aye, but my blessing still stands. I have seen the way you look at my daughter, Alexander. The love you two bear for each other cannot be refuted. I understand you have your duty and honor, and they dictate every decision you make. I was young once too, lad." The laird sat back, running his hand absently over his beard, his gaze steady. "When you leave my lands and make your way south, be sure to stop and see your family."

"What purpose would it serve?" Alexander asked, although he could not deny the idea of seeing his mother and sisters again made his heart a bit lighter.

"Seeing one's family has a way of making one reevaluate their priorities." The laird relayed the words of wisdom much like a father would to a son. "Speak to them, take the time to let them see you with Madeline, and then let my daughter decide if she will choose you for herself."

Alexander nodded, unsure of what to say in response. The laird had it the right of it: family had a way of setting him on the right path. Normally he discussed what weighed on his mind with Gabriel. He felt uncomfortable taking Madeline to wife without voicing his concerns aloud to someone who understood him. His mother would be the only other person with whom he could bear his heart in such a way. It would be the perfect opportunity for both him and Madeline. Until then, he would do the honorable thing and wait to tell Madeline of his intentions.

The laird spoke again, shaking him from his thoughts. "If Douglas or McLairn take it in their mind to seek you out, they will not hesitate to kill you. They believe you have caused them injury by stealing Madeline away. Which will be true, in a sense, once you leave this place."

Alexander understood the implication now. Once he left the keep with Madeline, it did not matter why. Those two men would hold him accountable for their injured pride. He shook his head.

"To the eyes of those here at this tournament, you will have stolen away with their possible prize. All I can do is offer compensation and mitigate the damage. 'Tis my own fault," the laird said with a soft chuckle. "Thinking I could use my daughter in such a way. I had not known how like her mother she would become. Headstrong and independent, unwilling to be used as a pawn in the games of politics. I have brought this on myself, and I shall deal with the consequences. All I ask is you care for her, keep her safe, and make her happy."

Alexander could not speak. His mind raced, being pulled into two different directions at once. He wanted to be sure he was what Madeline truly wanted, what she deserved in a husband. Deep in his heart he knew, she would always be the only woman who could complete him.

"On my honor, I will protect her with my life."

The day passed quickly, and Madeline spent most of it preparing for her journey. A mixture of anticipation and excitement swirled deep inside of her. She fell asleep while waiting for her father to fetch her. A soft knock at the door roused her from sleep.

She climbed from the bed and crossed the room. As she opened the door, Angus stood there, dressed in black, his sword strapped to his back. Her return to the Baron of Rayne, leaving her family again, the night in the cave, everything came to her in a rush of emotion.

"Are you ready, Kitten?"

With a nod, Madeline snatched her bag off the bed and followed Angus down the hall. Her father had not told her who would be taking her back to the baron, but it was only fitting the one who fetched her would be the one who returned her. She stopped, remembering one important detail.

"What about Heather?"

"She is already waiting with the horses," he said, exasperation clear in his voice. "The daft lass will not cease her jabbering."

It sounded like her sister had recovered enough to travel. She checked in on her earlier in the day. The girl had been up and moving around, bouncing off the chamber walls. Her arm had been bandaged and tucked in a sling across her chest, although it hardly ever stayed still. It seemed as though the pain bothered her little. She swung her arm around, animated as she asked Madeline a hundred questions. *How long would the journey take? Would they encounter any bandits along the way? Was Alexander coming with them?* It had taken Madeline until dinner to calm her sister to the point where she could answer her questions.

They had made her wonder about Alexander. What had her father said to him? She worried her lip. Had he told her father of their night together? Would they be forced to marry? Part of her hoped they would, and then she could finally have him as her husband. She scoffed. Would it not be fitting for them to have to marry out of duty and honor, since it led them both to this moment in the first place?

They slipped down the stairs and out through the kitchen. She followed Angus into the bailey. Four horses waited for them. Heather was mounted on her sturdy highland pony. Alexander stood holding his black destrier and her dappled gelding.

A flood of relief and elation washed over her. Alexander was joining them. Did her father ask him to come along? To guide them? She glanced around the deserted bailey. It seemed as though none of her questions would be answered.

Alexander stepped forward, offering a hand to help her into the saddle. His hand steadied her hip as she pulled herself up onto the horse's back. A flutter of awareness shot through her, and she glanced at him. His eyes betrayed nothing in the lantern light, and his mouth was set in a thin line, as if he were concentrating on a task. When she settled safely atop her mount, he handed her the reins and stepped away, quickly moving to mount his own horse.

"Stay close and stay quiet," Angus said, turning in his saddle to make sure they were ready. "Let us ride." He led them out the postern gate and down the field, away from the encampment and the village. They would have to go around the long way to avoid being seen.

Madeline rode behind him silently. Alexander followed after Heather, taking up the rear. They followed the edge of the forest to keep them hidden and rode until the keep slowly receded in the distance.

The full moon lit their path. She glanced toward the heavens. The starlight twinkled next to the pale moon, not a cloud in the sky. They had reached the bottom of the hill outside the village before the shouts rang out through the valley. A band of men appeared on the hill near the encampment, torches blazing in their hands.

Angus glared over his shoulder. "We need to run," he said as he urged his horse into a gallop. The valley leveled out, a flat expanse of open field in front of them. They needed to make it beyond the village and into the forest before whoever had spotted them decided to set chase. Madeline dug her heels into the horse's flanks and prayed Heather could keep up.

They broke into an open glen and ran until they reached the safe cover of the forest. Madeline's heart pounded in her chest. The exhilaration of the moment faded as the horses slowed to a walk. The horses panted, and the soft plodding of their hooves in the dirt echoed through the trees.

Madeline glanced at Heather, who rode just ahead of her. Even with her arm in a sling, the lass rode better than many children her own age. A surge of pride welled up inside her. Evelyn would love her. The thought of her cousin made her heart long for her friend, someone to help her unravel the tangled mess in her mind.

She could freely choose the man she wanted, but Alexander's actions confused her. Alexander had distanced himself again, as he had back at her uncle's keep. Madeline wondered if she had done something to upset him, to make him not want her. Perhaps he held a grudge against her for making him walk back to her father's castle through ankle deep mud. She giggled. He had looked rather adorable covered in mud and dirt.

With a glance over her shoulder, she met his gaze. He watched her without a hint of humor in his expression. Madeline smiled at him, and, for a brief moment, she believed he might return the gesture. Alas, with an incline of his head, he turned his attention to the forest around them. It seemed as though her stoic knight had returned, duty and honor shrouding him once again. With a sigh, she turned from him and pondered ways to make him see her as he had the evening before.

They rode most of the night, stopping to rest in the forest and then continuing on the next day. The group approached a small village, the smoke from the cluster of buildings luring them with the promise of a good meal and a warm, soft bed. They stopped outside the stables. Angus paid a few coins, and they left their horses to rest properly.

"Come," Angus said, gesturing to follow him.

Heather slipped her hand into Madeline's. Her heart fluttered as Alexander lingered a moment with the stable boy. Did he truly realize what he did to her, the dreams for which he made her long? He caught her gaze. She turned away, her pace quickening as they approached the inn.

Angus spoke with the innkeeper. The tavern seemed small but clean. At least they would be able to sleep in a bed and eat a warm meal. Madeline led Heather to sit down at one of the tables. There were no other travelers. She turned when the door opened, and Alexander stepped inside. Her heart did a little flip every time he walked into the room, or came close to her, or looked at her. She sighed.

"Are you well, Maddy?" Heather's concerned voice broke her reverie.

"Aye, my love." Madeline shifted in her seat as Alexander joined them.

He glanced at Angus and then took in the room with a steady perusal. Finally, his gaze landed on Heather.

"How fares your arm, lass?" His baritone slid over her like butter on warm bread.

"Och, it itches something fierce." Heather tugged her

bandaged arm against the sling.

"Stop pulling on it like that," Madeline admonished. She caught Alexander's lip quirking in a smile. It defied logic, the way he made her feel. She never imagined she could be more enamored of him than she had been before this whole mess started.

"I broke my arm once," Alexander said to Heather.

Heather's face lit up. She leaned toward him conspiratorially. "What happened? Did you get attacked by a bear?"

"Nay, nothing so dramatic. 'Twas quite silly, actually. My brother and I were fighting with wooden swords, and he caught me with my guard down."

Madeline felt her heart warming all over again. She had to remind herself to keep her distance. Even though her father told her she did not have to marry any of the suitors, his approval of Alexander had not been given either. Exhaustion settled over her, and she wanted nothing more than to fill her belly with a hearty meal and go to sleep.

Angus joined them, plopping down on a chair between Madeline and Alexander.

"Well," he said. "I have secured us three rooms for the evening. There are no other guests here tonight. I have requested our meals and a bath for you and Heather." Angus motioned to Madeline.

A bath sounded like heaven. They had ridden hard and slept in the forest. Her hair needed untangling and the dirt smeared across her face and neck needed removal.

"If you would be so kind, Angus." Madeline stood. "Have them bring my meal to my room. If we are to continue on in the morning, then I should retire early."

"Aye." Angus nodded. "You should go with her, wee hellion."

Heather stuck her tongue out at him as she reluctantly stood. Angus mimicked her. Madeline rolled her eyes, a grown man who acted worse than a ten year old child. She shook her head.

"Come along, my love." Madeline held her hand out. Heather slid hers into it. Alexander's blue eyes followed her every movement.

A stout woman approached them carrying a tray of food. "Here you are," she said, setting the tray down.

"Would you mind bringing ours up to our room?" Madeline asked her as she set the trenchers in front of Alexander and Angus.

"Aye, my dear." She hefted the tray with the remaining food and walked toward the stairs. "Come along then. I shall take you up straight away."

Leaving her brother and Alexander to their meals, she turned and followed the woman up the stairs. With one last glance over her shoulder, she caught Alexander's intense stare. A shiver of desire rippled through her. If he could paralyze her with just a look, imagine what he could do...Madeline shook her head. Such thoughts were inappropriate and would only make her more miserable.

They ascended the stairs, and the woman unlatched the door then pushed it open with her ample hip.

"Here you are then, my dears." She stepped into the room and slid the tray onto a small table by the window.

Madeline nodded. "Gra'mercy." She set her bag down on the bed.

"My name is Ellie. Do not hesitate to ask for anything." Ellie bustled toward the door. "I shall send up the bath straight away." She pulled the door closed behind her, leaving Madeline and Heather alone in the room.

It suited their needs. The linens were well worn but clean. Heather sat down and devoured her supper.

"Ywou shoulfd eeat," Heather said with her mouth stuffed full to bursting. She swallowed the mouthful. "You have to be hungry."

"I am." Madeline sat down next to her and broke off a piece of bread. She dipped it into the stew and took a bite. Her stomach growled. She had not realized just how hungry she was until then. They ate in silence until a knock sounded at the door.

"Enter." Madeline turned to see several servants carrying a wooden tub. They set it down and filled it as Madeline and Heather ate. By the time their food was eaten, their bath waited for them, steaming and inviting.

"You go first, Heather," Madeline insisted, tugging on her little sister's hand.

"But I do not want to take a bath," she whined.

"You are covered in dirt and your hair needs washing." Madeline jerked the stubborn child to her feet and pulled her clothes off. "Into the tub."

Heather grumbled as she stepped into the hot water careful to keep her injured arm perched on the edge of the tub as she settled in the water. Madeline picked up the soap the servants left, along with some clean linens to dry off with, and scrubbed the layers of dirt from her sister's face and hair.

"Do you love him?" Heather's question startled Madeline.

"Who, my love?" Madeline asked, trying to sound natural. Inside her heart raced, and her mind screamed.

"Alexander," Heather said, turning toward her. "Do not play coy with me, Maddy. You have not stopped staring at him since you first saw him." Madeline did not say anything; she just washed the girl's hair, untangling knots as she did so. "I would not blame you. He is quite handsome and strong." Heather paused. "And he has a gorgeous bum."

"*Heather!*" Madeline gaped at her sister's comments, shocked at their implications. "Have you been spying on him in his private moments?"

Heather shrugged. They sat in silence as she helped her little sister bathe and braided her clean hair. Once she finished, Madeline gave her a fresh shift to wear and tucked her into the bed.

She picked up Heather's clothing and draped it over the chair. When she glanced back at the bed, Heather's eyes were closed. Her soft breaths indicated the wee lass had already fallen asleep. With a sigh, Madeline removed her gown and shift.

As she sank into the water, the heat enveloped her like a warm embrace. She sighed. Her thoughts wandered to Alexander as she lathered her body with soap. She could not deny how much she wanted him.

If she appeared before him, naked and dripping wet, what would he do? Would he deny her his touch? Could she even be so bold? Dipping beneath the water, she rinsed the wicked desires away. The safest place for her was in bed, asleep, not chasing fantasies of a man she would never have because he remained too stubborn to take her for his own.

Chapter Fifteen

After devouring their supper, Angus and Alexander sat in the common room of the tavern. The innkeeper's wife, Ellie, had taken away their empty mugs, replacing them with full ones. Angus nursed his. It did nothing to ease the worry settling in the pit of his stomach. He glanced at Alexander, who had not even touched his second ale.

"You have been quiet since we left the keep." Angus' words cut the silence. "Something on your mind, Alexander?"

"Nay." Alexander took a drink.

Angus studied him, his expression shuttered. He liked the man who sat across from him, but there were times when Angus was not convinced Alexander had been completely forthright with him.

"You have been brooding since I found you in the cave with my sister," he said. "Have you been dwelling on what my father said?"

Alexander drained the rest of the ale in one swallow. Angus arched his brow.

"Slow down, you will drown yourself." Angus sat back in his chair, stretching his legs out, and changed the subject. "Do you think your mother will be glad to see you?"

"Aye." Alexander set the mug down.

"And your sisters?"

"What of them?" Alexander's gaze narrowed on Angus.

"Are they married?" Angus asked, a smirk playing on his lips. When he had learned Alexander had two sisters living with his mother, he could not resist heckling the stoic knight.

"You will not touch them," Alexander's tone darkened. "Do not speak to them, do not look at them."

"I encouraged your unspoken desire to chase after my sister." Angus pressed his hand to his heart. "I caught you kissing her and did nothing. I found you both sleeping with your arms and legs tangled up like a lovers' knot. And. I. Did. Nothing." He punctuated the last few words for emphasis. "I am wounded you hold me in such low esteem."

Alexander sighed, pushing the mug away. "You had every right to tell me to stop pining after your sister, to hit me when I kissed her, to string me up from the nearest tree when you found us together in the cave." His gaze met Angus', and he shook his head. "You trusted me when you had no reason to do so."

"You can tell me what is going on in that thick English skull of yours," Angus said, finishing his ale and setting the mug down. He moved to speak when the door of the inn swung open, revealing a cloaked figure in the doorway.

Alexander and Angus both glanced up. The figure in red closed the door and then pulled a hood back to reveal expertly coiffed black hair, studded with tiny pearl pins.

The room temperature escalated, causing Angus to shift in his seat. He needed another drink. The woman scouted the room. Her gaze passed over the two of them briefly. Angus' heart stopped. She looked like an angel, like a fairy from the stories he heard as a child.

"Angus." The voice sounded distant to his ears. He barely heard Alexander say his name.

The innkeeper came out of the back room, shuffling up to the beautiful stranger, keeping their conversation hushed. Angus caught himself leaning toward them, then straightened and met Alexander's gaze. A half smile hung on the knight's lips.

"What?" Angus shrugged. He picked up his mug and glanced down into the empty cup. "Damn." He set it down with more force than necessary and all attention shifted to him. He felt the heat creeping up his neck.

Ellie bustled over to their table, wiping her hands on her apron. "Can I get you some more ale?" she asked, gathering the empty mugs.

"I will have another," Angus said quickly, his gaze slipping past her to the woman in red.

Alexander put his hand up and shook his head. Ellie turned and walked back to the kitchen.

"I am for bed." Alexander stood and glanced down at Angus. "Stay out of trouble." He turned and headed for the stairs, leaving Angus sitting alone.

Ellie returned with his ale and set it down. "Will you be needing anything else, my dear?" she asked, her ruddy cheeks glowing.

Angus shook his head, and she left him. The innkeeper accepted a few coins from the woman and gestured for her to sit down. Her gaze focused on Angus. She crossed the space between them, stopping beside his table.

"Will your friend be returning?" she asked, her foreign accent wrapping around him. It sounded decidedly French.

"Nay," he said, standing. "Would you care to join me?" He pointed to the table. She nodded, and he pulled out a chair for her. "You are traveling through here then?" Angus winced at how stupid his question sounded. *Of course she is traveling, you dunce.* "I mean, your accent, you are not from Scotland. Are you?" Not quite as stupid but barely an improvement. He would not be surprised if she walked away.

"*Non,*" she replied, pulling the gloves from her fingers and laying them on the table.

"Do you have a name?" Angus asked. She was playing coy with him, only offering select pieces of information. He grinned.

"Jacqueline." Her husky voice sent a shiver of lust rippling through his body.

He shook his head to shake the inappropriate images forming in his mind.

"Do you have a name?" Jacqueline parroted. Her slender fingers loosened the clasp at her neck, and she slipped the cloak from her shoulders, draping over the back of her chair. The dark blue gown emphasized her bright eyes as they focused on him alone.

"Angus," he replied, his tongue darting out to wet his lips. He picked up the ale and drank. Bloody hell, he had just met this woman, and already she had him harder than an ancient oak.

"Angus," she murmured her voice breathy. The way she said his name made him feel like a ten-year-old lad who had just caught a glimpse of his first naked woman. She leaned her elbows on the table and interlaced her hands, cradling her chin in them. Her eyes were a whisky colored amber. "Are you here with your wife?"

He forgot to breathe. "Nay," he replied, swallowing the lump in his throat. His palms were sweaty, his heart racing. *Christ, what is wrong with me?* He had never been this way around a woman, ever. He did not mention Madeline and Heather. She could have assumed Alexander was another traveler who had chosen to sup with a stranger.

"Here you are, my dear," Ellie said, setting down a trencher of stew and a mug of ale in front of Jacqueline.

Angus jumped at her sudden appearance. He squirmed in his seat and finished the tankard, thrusting it toward Ellie.

"Another one then, lad?" she asked with a knowing smile. He had not even answered when she scuttled off.

Jacqueline picked at the bread, dipping it delicately into the stew broth. She brought it to her lips. It touched her tongue, and Angus lost all train of thought.

"Why is a lovely lass like you traveling alone?" He leaned forward, meeting her gaze.

She chewed and swallowed, matching his intensity, her whisky eyes unflinching. "Why do you care?" she asked, her tone sweet as honeyed mead, but he sensed the challenge beneath it.

"Can a man not be concerned for a lady's safety?"

"I am perfectly capable of defending myself," she replied, taking another bite.

"I have heard that before," Angus scoffed. He heard Madeline speak often of Evelyn and their cousin's insistence on being able to protect herself. It obviously worked out well, since she had been kidnapped. "Women think they can take care of themselves, until they cross the wrong man's path." He raised his hands in punctuation of his words.

"I am not like most women." Jacqueline sipped her ale. She wrinkled her nose at the taste and then shook her head, tracing her finger around the rim of the tankard. "I know how to defend myself." She pushed the mug toward him.

"Ale not to your taste?" Angus chuckled at her reaction. Slim and petite, she would never be able to hold a sword against a man his size. Her pale skin, black hair, and bewitching eyes set her apart from every woman in Scotland. She stood out like a black sheep in a sea of white ones. "Come now, you do not expect me to believe that?"

Jacqueline finished chewing and swallowed. She licked each finger in turn, sliding her tongue over her fingertips.

Oh, bloody fucking hell. He could not have looked away if he wanted to. She had mesmerized him. Pure torture. His groin ached, and he sat up straighter. What was it about this woman that drove him to the point where he could not even think clearly? He picked up her mug of ale and downed it in one swallow.

Jacqueline stood and closed the distance between them. Sliding her hand in his, she pulled him out of his seat.

"Come with me." Her sultry voice booked no argument. He followed her as she led him into a small chamber off the main room. Closing the door behind them, she turned to face him.

"What—"

Her fingertip pressed against his lips, effectively silencing him. He slid his tongue across her fingertip and drew it into his mouth. She tasted sweet, like a confection. Her hand slid into his hair, and she pulled his head down, crushing her lips to his.

Startled by the sudden onslaught, Angus quickly recovered and returned the kiss. He had kissed dozens of women before, but none had tasted so sweet, so forbidden, so natural as she did. He cradled her neck in his hands, feeling the softness of her skin.

Jacqueline sighed against his mouth. A tiny moan escaped her, getting tangled in the heat of their kiss. Her hands roamed down over his shoulders, sliding along the folds of his plaid. She pressed herself against him, wanting the contact as much as he did.

"Lass," he murmured between frantic kisses. "What have you done to me?" His words slurred with every breath. The room began to spin.

"Just let it take you," she whispered as he leaned heavily

against her. She slowly eased him to the ground, where he collapsed in a heap against the wall.

"Take me?" he mumbled. She knelt next to him. His eyelids grew heavy, and he struggled to keep them open.

"Shhh." Jacqueline pressed a kiss to his head. "Go to sleep, Angus, darling," the fairy whispered as he lost consciousness.

Chapter Sixteen

Alexander lay in bed, staring at the ceiling. He recognized the expression on Angus' face when the woman in red walked into the inn. She had cast her seductive net over his friend, and Alexander could not help but shake his head. There had been a moment where he had been concerned for the hearts of his sisters, but after seeing Angus' besotted look, he believed his concern for his sisters was no longer warranted. Bowing out of the room had been the smartest thing he had done in weeks. No reason to get entangled in Angus' affairs now.

The fire crackled in the hearth. Darkness filtered through the window. He needed to get some rest. Sleep had avoided him since the night in the cave, as if he could not sleep without Madeline in his arms. He shifted onto his side, punching the pillow flat before laying his head down on the linen.

His mind drifted to the woman sleeping in the room beside his own. Part of him wanted to go to her, but he knew she shared the room with Heather. The little hellion would probably stick her dagger through his heart if he dared to disturb them. Any journey would prove difficult, even more so for an injured child. Heather had proved to be quite resilient. He had yet to hear a complaint from her.

He closed his eyes, willing sleep to come. A sharp rap at the door snapped him out of the half conscious state. Grumbling, he pushed himself off the bed and walked over to the door. *If Angus has come to cry to me about his failed wooing, so help me, I will thrash him.* Alexander lifted the latch and swung the wooden door open.

Madeline stood before him in naught but her shift. He thought he might be dreaming, but she pushed past him and entered his room without a word. Alexander shut the door and turned to face her.

"I could not sleep," she confessed, her hands twisting the fabric of her shift. "Heather has taken up the center of the bed and mumbles in her sleep."

Alexander stared at her. A desperate part of him wanted to ask her to share the bed with him. He shook the fantasies from his head and retained what little shred of honor remained somewhere inside of him.

"You can sleep here if you would like," he offered, seeing the exhausted look on her face. Her fingers fidgeted with the end of the loose braid hanging over her shoulder. Madeline's gaze strayed everywhere, except his face.

"Where will you sleep?" she asked, her gaze finally meeting his.

A spark of heat ignited somewhere inside of his chest and burned straight to his groin. He wished he could be like Gabriel and take a chance, but he had a code by which he lived and would not break it. No matter how much he wanted to take her in his arms. That night in the cave had been close, too close. He had kicked himself for it afterward.

"I shall sleep on the chair." He gestured to the rickety wooden chair in the corner of the room. "Or the floor. Where I sleep does not matter to me." He shrugged, trying to be casual. Normally he could sleep anywhere, but tonight, knowing Madeline slept in his bed and he could not be with her, he would never get any rest.

Madeline walked a few steps closer. He could feel the heat radiating from her body through the thin linen shift. Alexander bit his tongue to keep from speaking, from groaning, anything that would betray his desire for her.

"You could sleep with me," she whispered, her gold-flecked eyes boldly meeting his.

"It would not be appropriate." He balled his hands into fists at his side to keep from reaching for her.

"It would not be the first time." She drew her bottom lip between her teeth, watching him. Her hand trailed down over the folds of the plaid crossing his chest. The back of her fingers caressed his chest through his shirt, leaving his body burning and aching in its wake.

"Madeline." He snatched her wrist as she trailed lower to

his waist. "You cannot ask me to do this. The cave..." He struggled to find the right words. "That night was a mistake."

She jerked her hand from his grasp as if he had just struck her.

"It was not a mistake," she hissed, turning away from him. "You daft fool."

He immediately regretted his words. Would he never be able to communicate with her? Gabriel had been right. He was terrible with words.

"Maddy," he said, slipping his hand around her arm. He turned her to face him. Her cheeks were damp with tears. She wiped them away hastily.

"Do not dare judge me, Alexander." She thrust her chin up and sniffed.

"Judge you for what?" he asked. Her cheeks flushed with a rosy pink, the color of her eyes enhanced by the tears.

"For wanting to be with you," she whispered.

His heart stilled at her confession. He could not deny he felt the same way, but to acknowledge it would make him force his hand before he spoke to his family. Once he reached his mother's home then he would be able to make a rational decision.

"I know you want me." Her voice grew stronger with each word. "You cannot hide the hunger in your eyes when you look at me."

The bold statement made him hard as an anvil. Saints alive, he struggled to contain himself. She pressed her body against his, draping her hands over his shoulders. The last threads of his self-control unraveled as she threaded her fingers through his hair.

"*Mo cridhe,*" she murmured as she pulled his head down and pressed her lips to his.

Alexander swore as he wrapped his arms around her, jerking her against him.

The door swung open with a shudder, slamming into the wall. They jumped, abruptly ending the kiss. Alexander dropped his hands from Madeline and took a step back as he glanced at the door.

Angus stood in the doorway, leaning heavily against the frame. His gaze lingered on Alexander then shifted to Madeline. His pale face grew red.

"What in the bloody hell is going on in here?" Angus shouted, stepping into the room.

"I can explain." Madeline stepped between them, intercepting her brother before he could be within arm's reach of Alexander.

"Madeline, what are you doing in his room in the middle of the night?" Angus tilted her chin up.

Alexander backed up, giving them space. He crossed his arms and waited silently. *How could I have let it happen again?* Her scent intoxicated him. Her words wove a seductive web around him. He rubbed his hand across his face. He would be lucky if he escaped this night without incurring a black eye or a broken nose.

"What I do is none of your business, Angus Campbell." She jabbed a finger in his chest. Alexander bit back a laugh. With a flounce, she pushed past her brother and returned to her own room.

Alexander did not know whether to be relieved she had left or concerned she had left him alone with Angus, who looked as though he would throttle the next person who crossed him. Unfortunately, the next person happened to be Alexander.

"So you think you can just take advantage of my sister whenever you damned well please?" Angus stepped toward him, a wicked gleam in his eye. "I guess you have made a decision then concerning my sister's future."

"Nay," Alexander replied, standing his ground. He had never backed away from a fight a day in his life. He would not cower, nor would he run. He always faced his challenges head on. Angus appeared bent on murder. "Nothing happened, Angus. I swear to you on my father's grave. I will do my duty to your sister, once we reach my mother's home." He did not feel it necessary to inform Angus of his sister's seductive actions and his inability to deny their effect on him.

Angus stood before him, his hands clenched so tightly they

were white. "She stole my coin." Angus mumbled so quietly, Alexander hesitated, unsure if he had heard him correctly.

"Who?"

"The woman in the red cloak. Jacqueline." Angus paced to the far side of the room, then back again. He repeated the motion as he spoke. "She bewitched me, damn it."

Alexander arched a brow. *How had a slip of a woman like her overpowered Angus enough to take his coin?* Then the realization dawned on him.

"She seduced you?" Alexander asked slowly, not wanting to stir his ire any more than necessary.

"Aye," he snapped, muttering incoherent swear words beneath his breath. "I am an arse." His laugh held no mirth. "I should have seen it coming."

"What happened?" Alexander raised his brow, curious. She did not look like a thief, more like a noble woman draped in such an extravagant color.

"The witch poisoned me," Angus grumbled.

Alexander could not control the laughter as it burst from his lips.

"I fail to see the humor in this." Angus glowered at him.

"My apologies." Alexander bit his lip, and the pain helped to quell the desire to laugh. "If she poisoned you, would you not be dead?"

"She gave me something which put me to sleep." He walked over to the window and glanced out. The dim light of dawn intermingled with the reluctant grip of night.

"When was this?" Alexander asked.

"Just after you left."

Alexander nodded. "It would be best if we did not mention this to your sisters." He picked up his sword and fastened it onto his back. "Perhaps it would be best if we readied the horses and left as soon as possible."

Angus glanced at him. "Aye. The sooner we reach your family's home, the safer we will be. At least then we might be able to get some rest without being accosted."

Alexander bit his lip again as Angus walked past him and

out the door. The poor bastard was in for a rude awakening when he met Alexander's mother and sisters. They made Heather seem like a sister of the cloth.

Chapter Seventeen

Madeline jerked her gown on, fastening the laces as best she could without her sister's help. Of all the moments Angus could have chosen to storm into someone's room, he chose that one. She exhaled sharply. It had taken her most of the night to work up the courage to go to Alexander. He had been avoiding her, finding excuses to keep a distance between them. After the night in the cave, she thought they had finally come to an understanding. Sufficiently frustrated, Madeline tied the laces with an exasperated breath.

She could not do anything about it now. The moment ended, and she wanted to strangle her brother for once again having the worst timing imaginable. She gave up on the laces, letting them drop, and sat on the edge of the bed to pull on her boots.

Heather shifted, mumbling, yet again, in her sleep. The girl must be having bad dreams. She shushed her softly then glanced up at the window. A soft ray of sunrise peeked through the glass. She stood and walked over to the ledge.

Two men approached the inn leading four horses. She watched them for a moment. The taller one pointed to the inn, and the other man entered the building.

Madeline gathered her bag and tucked her brush into it. A soft knock echoed in the small chamber. She rushed to the door and opened it a crack. Angus stood there, his cheeks flushed with exertion.

"Wake Heather, gather your things, and meet us downstairs as soon as you are ready." He turned away without waiting for her reply. She shut the door and woke Heather.

Silently, the sisters collected their belongings and slipped from the room. When they walked outside, Madeline blinked against the sun's light as it broke over the horizon. Angus helped Heather onto her horse.

Madeline mounted her gelding, stealing a glance at Alexander who sat atop his horse waiting for them. He sat straight and tall in the saddle, his gaze everywhere but on Madeline. She sighed. Once again, she cursed Angus and his impeccable timing.

When they were all ready, Alexander led them south from the small village. Madeline stared at Alexander's back as they rode. She wanted to talk to him, but she feared there was no point. A glance over her shoulder revealed Heather taking in the scenery with wide eyes and a silly grin. At least someone had gotten some rest.

Madeline shook her head. Poor girl believed this to be quite a grand adventure. She had prattled on about being captured by bandits or pirates or the English. The stories grew bolder with every moment that passed. Nothing Madeline said to her sister would convince her of the truth. Not one even remotely exciting thing would happen to them, especially the bit with the pirates, since they were so far from the sea.

They rode for a bit when Alexander slowed his mount, bringing their horses side by side. He said nothing, just kept his eyes on the road before them. Madeline enjoyed the scenery, the rolling hills, the patches of forest dotting the hillsides, and the streams as they snaked their way through the valleys.

It hurt watching him, but knowing he rode right beside her and said nothing irritated her more than the incessant whistling behind them. She turned and glared at Angus, who shrugged and pursed his lips again in a tuneless whistle. Madeline scowled at him, wanting to scream.

"I wanted to apologize," Alexander said, his voice low. "About what happened."

Startled, she glanced at him. "There is no reason to apologize, sir," she said in a casual tone, as if his attention truly meant nothing to her. Madeline was enjoying the anger simmering beneath the surface. It made her feel alive and reckless.

His ice blue eyes met hers, his hair falling across his brow. He ran his hand through the locks. Madeline looked away quickly, her heart racing. Just seeing his fingers thread through his hair turned her to marmalade. She did not trust her voice. Her fingertips itched to touch his silky hair again, as she had in the wee hours of the morning.

"Madeline," he said, his voice melting over her like honey on a fresh tart. "You and I must speak. There are some things you must know."

She nodded, avoiding his eyes. *Speak? About what? What does he wish to tell me? He was a fool and should have taken me when I offered myself?* Her heart raced as she anticipated his words. She swallowed hard, waiting for him to continue.

"My family," he began.

Her hopes fell at his words. He wanted to speak about his family.

"My sisters and even my mother, they can be a bit overly dramatic and quite meddling."

"Dramatic and meddling?" Madeline parroted. *What is he trying to say?* She shrugged her shoulders. "Makes no difference to me, I harmonize with everyone. Perhaps I shall have a long conversation with your mother about your lack of manners and the blatant lapse in your ability to communicate clearly." She grinned at him, allowing a little bit of sarcasm to creep into her voice. "Are you afraid they will betray all your secrets, Alexander? That they will tell me who you really are behind the stony façade you wear so well."

Alexander stared at her. "You think you are prepared for this," he said slowly. "I have naught to hide."

Madeline thought a moment as a smirk threatened to overtake her lips. "For some reason, I do not believe you. I am sure they have some interesting stories to tell about the lad you once were."

Alexander gave her a sharp look and urged his horse into a run. Madeline followed suit, as did Angus and Heather. His cryptic words made her more excited to meet his family. They lingered in her mind as they galloped down the south road, the wind blowing her hair. *Finally, some answers.*

Sunset encroached upon the band of riders. They had been on the road for two days and checked every possible route they could have taken.

He brooded, beyond irritated at this point. The small village had been the one they had not checked. All the others had proved failures. He kicked his horse into a canter, pulling to a stop as they reached the small inn. A dozen men barely made an intimidating crew, but he took what he could get. There had been no time to round up the rest of his men.

Laird Campbell had been none too pleased with his demands when he left the keep a few days ago. The tournament had been nothing but a ruse to ferret him out. He swore. When he had discovered the information, it threw him into a rage. He should have known by the meticulous organization of the event.

Well, old man Campbell had been so surprised when he realized who had been stealing from under his nose for the last few years. It almost pained him not to revel in the laird's reaction. Unfortunately for the head of the Campbell clan, he had taken certain precautions before he left. Two of his men had returned to his own clan and warned them of the potential consequences of the failed tournament. If the laird took it upon himself to hunt them down, he would not know where to look. His own father knew nothing of his plans or his intentions. Just as he had hoped.

With a grin, he nodded to one to his men. The burly lad climbed down off his horse and barged into the inn. It felt quite nice to such control over his men. He enjoyed tormenting and pillaging as much as the next bandit, but, until this moment, he had to be careful of how he did so. The laird knew who he was and what his plans were, no need for discretion now. Shouting commenced, along with the sound of wood breaking.

He sat on his horse, scanning the street and the buildings lining it. What a shame most people did not just cooperate with him. Life would have been so much simpler. He was not a difficult man to figure out. He wanted his due: nothing more, nothing less. He spotted a small stable where the road bent to leave town. He debated on whether they should stay there for the night and rest, but they were so close, he could feel it. Taking any time to rest now would give the Campbells more of a lead. He spat.

Adjusting the plaid across his shoulder, he re-centered the brooch above his heart, if he even had a heart. He whistled low as he waited. It felt almost refreshing to be unencumbered by the deception keeping him hidden from the laird. After years of manipulation, of hiding, he could finally stand proud of his accomplishments.

A few moments later, the henchman returned, his hair mussed from the fight. The soft echo of a woman crying reached his ears. He brushed the annoyance aside.

"What news have you?" he asked, irritated and slightly impatient.

"They were here last night, my laird." The man climbed back onto his horse and reined the beast around. "Headed south at dawn or so the innkeeper says."

"Good." He grinned. "Let us catch up with them, shall we?"

"Can we not stay here this eve?" one of the men asked.

"If you wish to keep your tongue, then *haud yer wheesht*," he snapped with a wave of his hand. "We must catch up with them before they reach the border."

"Malcolm." One of the shorter men came forward. "Go gather up some food for us to take on our journey." With a wicked smirk, the man slipped into the inn again, setting off a new bout of screams and tears.

He pinched the bridge of his nose. He should have known better. Madeline Campbell had been worth the right amount of money to make her a prize to any thief. He wondered if the bitch would be more of a nuisance than her worth in gold.

Taking a deep breath, he spun his horse around. "Take the other men and gather supplies." The man behind him nodded and spurred the others into action. He wearied of the games. Once he caught up with Madeline, he would finally be able to claim what should have been his.

Not killing her father outright stood out as the one regret lingering in the back of his mind. When he discovered she had gone, along with Alexander and Angus, he had stormed into the laird's presence chamber and confronted the old man. It had stunned him to say the least, but by then, pleasantries were no longer required. He had left the old man with a parting gift: a dagger through the palm and a promise. When he found Madeline, he would make her pay for her father's sins. He just hoped the *Sassenach* had not tainted her.

"We gathered everything we could carry," Malcom said upon his return, the rest of his men slowly circled around him, loading the bounty into the bags tied to their saddles.

"Very well. Onward men!" He urged his horse into a trot, eager to be on the move again. Leading the way out of town, he glanced over his shoulder. His men seemed fierce, ready to take on whatever they would encounter. *Good...they need to be prepared.* He turned his attention back to the road before him.

The sun dipped low on the horizon. They could make it a few miles before stopping for the night. It would not be long before he could revel in his revenge and taste the sweet victory of Madeline's lips. She would fight him, certainly, but he liked a woman who put up a bit of a struggle. It always made their surrender sweeter.

The sun had set hours ago, when a curling stream of smoke rising into the clear night caught her eye. *Finally.* She urged her horse faster, catching up to Alexander.

"Is that it?" Hope bubbled up inside of her.

"Aye," he said, shifting in his saddle. "Remember what I told you."

"You told me nothing." Madeline shot him a look of pure exacerbation. He was all riddles and no answers. Excitement built inside of her just to see a building, a place to eat, sleep, and be free of Alexander for a few minutes. His nearness plagued her, bringing all her senses to heightened awareness. His masculine scent mixed with horses and leather, and the sharp sting of his gaze on her when he thought her unaware. It damn near drove her to madness.

She had tried to keep her sister entertained as they rode along. Madeline even talked to Angus about the weather, but it seemed Angus was in a rather touchy mood as well. She wanted to talk to another woman for a change. She prayed his family would like her. Madeline desired their approval. Not as if it mattered, since Alexander seemed to have no intention of declaring for her hand in marriage. She scowled at him. *Infuriating man.*

They wove down from the hill into a small valley where the house stood. A stone home with a sturdy thatched roof, surrounded by gardens and pastures. Madeline grinned like a girl caught up in the beauty of her first spring celebration. She heard Alexander grunt beside her but refused to be deterred from her good mood.

As they approached the house, he slid from his saddle first and motioned for them to stay put. Madeline rolled her eyes and folded her arms across her chest.

He knocked on the door. A few moments passed before it opened, the tip of a blade pointed at his chest. The woman wielding it gasped with delight, dropping the sword to the wayside.

"*A chuilein,*" she said, wrapping her arms around Alexander.

"Mother." He picked her up and swung her around in a wide circle. When he set her on her feet again, his mouth curled in a boyish grin. "'Tis good to see you again."

"How could you stay away so long? We missed you." She glanced past him, spotting Madeline, then Heather and Angus. "We have company I see. Come in, my dears, come in." She pushed Alexander aside and approached Madeline as she climbed down from her horse.

Alexander grabbed the horses' reins. He and Angus led them to the pasture beside the house. Madeline slipped her hand into Heather's, and they approached the house.

"You can call me Bonnie." Alexander's mother wore a warm smile. She held a lantern up for them to enter the house. A fire crackled in the hearth. Even though it was not cold outside, it lent a homey warmth to the room, enough to make Madeline feel comfortable.

"You must be exhausted, *m'eudail*." Bonnie led them down the hall and pushed open a door to her right.

Madeline felt herself blush at the endearment. *My dear.* She could almost hear her mother's voice echoing in Bonnie's. Alexander's mother looked nothing like her own, but her demeanor was welcoming and warm as a mother's should be.

Bonnie motioned for them to follow her into the room. Heather and Madeline walked into the small bedroom. There were two beds on opposite walls.

"You can stay here tonight." Bonnie bent down to start a small fire in the hearth. "There is water over on the table, and I can fetch you some bread and cheese if you are hungry."

Heather collapsed on the bed closest to her with a relieved sigh.

"'Tis like sleeping on a cloud of angel hair," Heather said, her voice trailing off, entranced by the bliss of such a warm and welcoming bed.

Bonnie chuckled, coaxing the fire to life. It crackled and burned, slowly lending light to the room around them. Quite satisfied with her handiwork, she stood and picked up her lantern.

"Will you be needin' anything else, lass?" His mother turned to Madeline.

"Nay," Madeline said, clasping her hands together. "You have done more than enough for us. I thank you."

A curious smirk played on Bonnie's lips as she observed Madeline closely. "Just give a yell if you need anything. My room is just down the hall." She turned to leave and paused in the doorway. With a last glance over her shoulder, she smiled. "And do not let my daughters frighten you. I will make sure they leave you to rest."

With that cryptic remark, Bonnie left Madeline and Heather

to the comforts of their beds. One glance at Heather and she knew her little sister had already fallen asleep. Madeline removed her boots and covered the young girl with a blanket. She pressed a kiss to her forehead and set to undressing herself.

The warm embrace of the blankets lulled her into a dreamlike trance. Before she could ponder Bonnie's parting words again, she fell into a deep slumber filled with pleasant dreams featuring a brawny English knight.

Chapter Eighteen

Alexander stood next to the pasture. He had sent Angus inside, hoping his mother would find him a suitable bed for the night. He glanced up at the house. The moonlight played off the stone walls, casting much of it into shadows.

A hand on his shoulder startled him. He turned to gaze directly into the eyes of his mother.

"What trouble have you gotten into this time, *a chuilein*?" she asked, her brow knitted with concern.

"Och, Mother." He pushed away the ache in his chest. "'Tis nothing I cannot handle."

She chuckled. "You always say you can handle it, my son. You like to take on challenges, which often times are far too vast to deal with alone. 'Tis why the good Lord gave you a twin. Where is he anyway?"

Alexander sighed at the mention of Gabriel. He hated to have to be the bearer of such ill tidings.

"Mother," he began, fidgeting with his plaid. "We intercepted a plot against the Baron of Rayne. While we saved his life and the life of his daughter, Gabriel..." His voice trailed off. He truly did not know how to break the news to her. The last thing he knew, Gabriel had been alive but gravely injured.

She stared at him, her eyes wide, waiting for him to finish his words.

"Gabriel was injured in the attack. Lady Evelyn was caring for him when I left. She had high hopes for his recovery," he said. "But it has been over a fortnight since I have heard any news." He shrugged his shoulders. "I have no better news to give you."

Bonnie allowed herself a deep breath and exhaled slowly. Her eyes fluttered closed for a moment then met his again. "All will be well. The Lord works in mysterious ways." She crossed herself.

"He is in love," Alexander added. It seemed like an awkward moment for such news, but his mother deserved what little hope he had to offer.

Her eyes brightened, and a grin lit up her face. "Who is she?" Bonnie asked.

"Lady Evelyn Montgomery, daughter of the Baron of Rayne."

"My wild son has fallen for a lady of the court." She laughed. "I admit I find it difficult to imagine my Gabriel bending to the rules of the aristocracy in pursuit of a woman." She shrugged. "But love makes fools of us all."

Alexander cleared his throat of the lump forming there. Little did his mother know her remark hit far too close to home.

Her sharp eyes must have spotted his moment of weakness, and she honed in on it like an archer sighting a moving target.

"And what of you, Alexander?" She grinned. "Have you fallen into the fool's trap yourself?"

"Nay, mother," he said, shaking his head. His denial sounded weak, even to his own ears.

"'Tis the lovely lass you brought under my roof, is it not?" She offered a knowing wink. "You have never been able to lie well, Alexander."

He cringed at the truth of her statement. He was a horrible liar, which left him surprised he had been able to convince a castle full of highlanders he was another person completely. Her intense scrutiny persisted. Finally, he threw his hands up.

"All right, Mother. Aye...I love her. Are you satisfied?" He crossed his arms. Why was it so hard to admit the truth to his mother? *Because speaking the truth makes it real.* For so long, he dreamed of Madeline and what he wanted from her, with her. He feared speaking it would put them both in danger. The thought of any ill befalling her crushed his heart.

She laid a gentle hand on his arm. "What are you so afraid of, my son? That she does not love you?"

He shook his head. "Nay, 'tis more complicated."

"Tell me," she coaxed him, slipping her arm in his and leaning her head against his shoulder.

The warmth of her touch melted the last of his reserves. Since childhood, he ran to her when he needed comfort and a solution to his problems. Often times she merely listened, nodding and offering him comforting embraces. The fact someone cared enough to listen touched him and granted him a clear view of the situation.

"'Tis a long story," he murmured.

"Then let us go inside, and you can tell me all about her over a drink." She tugged him toward the stone building.

He nodded and followed her into the warmth of the house. His mother prepared a mug of warm spiced wine as he told her about the fool he had become and the woman who had stolen his heart.

A shrill scream pierced the silence. Madeline's eyes shot open, and she launched from the bed, blankets flying in a tangled heap through the air. She glanced at the empty bed where Heather had slept. She darted from the room and heard the scuffle as she ran down the hall.

Heather lay on the floor of the common room a large furry beast pinning her to the ground. Its long tangled hair hung down over the bulky body. The beast licked Heather's face, its large tongue leaving strings of slobber on her cheeks. The girl grinned and buried her fingers in the matted fur.

"Heather Campbell!" Madeline scolded. Heather ignored her and continued her panicked, breathless squealing as the dog laved her with attention.

A gentle cough sounded from behind her. Madeline turned to see Bonnie, Alexander, Angus, and two unfamiliar women seated at the long wooden table.

"Lass," Bonnie said, moving around the table to take her arm. "Mayhap you should dress before you join us to break your fast."

Madeline glanced down, and her face heated in a blaze. She

wore only a shift! She pulled away from Bonnie and quickly darted down the hall. Once she reached the room she and Heather had shared, she closed the door behind her and leaned against it. Madeline debated on whether or not it would be prudent to return to her bed, pull the covers over her head, and remain there for the rest of the day. Her face burned with embarrassment.

A soft knock startled her. She swallowed her wounded pride and opened the door a crack. Bonnie stood there, a pleasant expression on her face. "May I come in?"

Madeline stepped aside and opened the door. As Bonnie stepped into the room, Madeline studied Alexander's mother, petite with soft rounded curves. Her deep green eyes followed her with a twinkling curiosity. Bonnie's deep brown hair, a shade away from black with soft strands of gray woven through at her temples, belied her age. She did not look like a woman who had children as old as Alexander. *It must be quite a blessing to age with such grace.* She returned the woman's infectious smile.

"*Dinnea fash yersel,* lass." Bonnie gathered Madeline's hand into her own and patted the back. "I do not believe you have ruined your reputation." Her comforting remarks eased Maddy's conscience, although her cheeks were still warm with embarrassment.

"I assumed something had happened to Heather." Madeline sighed. "I might have overreacted a wee bit."

"Just a tad," Bonnie agreed with a laugh. "Come, dress yourself. I would like you to meet my daughters."

Madeline breathed a sigh of relief and nodded. Her cheeks still burned with embarrassment. Bonnie's eyes were kind and understanding.

"Tell me, Madeline, what are your thoughts on my son?" Bonnie sat on the edge of the bed.

"I am not sure what you mean." She pulled the kirtle on over her shift, tugging it into place.

"Come here and turn." Madeline moved closer, and Alexander's mother laced the strings on her gown. "It is obvious my son is smitten with you, yet you seem troubled."

Madeline exhaled a heavy breath. "'Tis nothing," she lied.

"Now, you do not expect me to believe that, do you?" Bonnie chuckled. "I have been around long enough to see the marks of love in both you and him."

"Your son is as stubborn as a jackass." The words spilled from her lips before she could stop them. "I beg pardon, my lady, my words were inappropriate."

Bonnie's laughter rang loud and clear in the small room. She finished tying the laces and wiped a tear from her eye. "Och, lass, you have the right of it. My son is just like his father, God rest his soul." She smoothed her hand over Madeline's skirt. "Do you love Alexander, despite his faults?"

"Aye." Madeline turned to the older woman. "I have loved him for a long while, although he never even acknowledged my existence." She hung her head. "I had believed he wanted me, but I may have been mistaken."

"What makes you say such a thing, lass?" Bonnie motioned for her to sit down, and she picked up a brush. Settling on the bed, Madeline basked in the loving attention as a daughter could receive from a mother. Her kind words and tender touch soothed Madeline's heart.

"Since we left my father's keep, Alexander has kept me at an arm's length." The gentle tug of the brush through her hair lulled her. "He confessed he loved me, but the next day, after he spoke to my father, he avoided me completely." She frowned, not realizing how much the distance between them had hurt her.

"Perhaps you should ask him what happened," Bonnie prompted as she braided Madeline's hair. "Ask him if his feelings for you have changed."

"I shall," Madeline said as courage balled in the pit of her stomach. "After I break my fast."

"Come then, let us go," Bonnie said, standing and pulling Madeline to her feet. "The girls have been asking after you."

"Gra'mercy, my lady. You have helped to ease my mind."

"'Twas naught, *m'eudail*." The older woman pulled her into a hug. "It will all work out, you will see." Pulling away, their eyes locked and then Bonnie turned, leaving Madeline alone in the room.

With a deep breath, she smoothed her hands down across her stomach and held them there, trying to calm the butterflies raging inside. Hopefully there would be a point where she could talk to Alexander alone. Bonnie's words stuck in the back of her mind. The only thing she could do was talk to him and find out what churned in his stubborn head. Madeline opened the door and, with her chin held high, walked down the hall toward a fate unknown.

The morning meal progressed better than Alexander expected. Angus had kept his eyes and his hands to himself. His sisters grew up with three older brothers, so it came as no surprise when they accepted him so quickly. He joined in the teasing and treated them as he would his own sisters.

Madeline. Seeing her burst into the common room wearing her shift made him ache for her. He wanted to wrap her into his arms and carry her back to his bed. It took all his willpower to sit there and not move, not speak. He knew Angus was watching him, awaiting a reaction. When she had retreated to her room, he speared her brother with a glance warning him of imminent death should he open his gob.

"Would you like some more to eat?" His mother stood next to him, a basket of rolls in her hand. "You barely touched your eggs." She tutted disapprovingly when he shook his head.

The warm sound of Madeline's laughter mingled with his sisters'. They had become quite close since she joined them at the table. His heart constricted as he watched her, like it was being squeezed in a meaty fist. He pushed away from the table and stood. Everyone turned toward him.

Madeline's rosy cheeks and bright eyes punched him in the gut. He needed to get some air before he did something ridiculous and impulsive, like kiss her in front of both his family and hers.

"I must check on the horses," he grumbled and walked out of the house without another word of explanation.

The sunlight blinded him for a moment. He raised his hand to block the sun's harsh glare. His horse whinnied at the sight of him. Stubborn beast had grown rather fond of his daily grain. Alexander shook his head and meandered over to the small shelter where the grain was kept. He sprinkled some in the feed bucket and began brushing the horse as he ate.

"What am I going to do now, Scar?" he murmured to the destrier. The beast shook his thick mane and dipped his head into the bucket again. "You are no help, you realize."

With every stroke of the brush, the horse's black coat shone like coal in the sunlight. The motions came naturally, and he became lost in thought. Angus knew the details of their mission, but up until this point he had not had a chance to discuss it with Madeline. His stomach roiled as he wondered if she would reject his plan. He would not force her to do anything, but he prayed she would agree to it.

"Have you been avoiding me?" Madeline's voice carried around the horse's body. She appeared near Scar's head, her hand gently stroking his muzzle as he chewed. "You have a wonderful family." Her words struck their mark, lodging deep in his heart.

"I thank you for your kind words," he said, draping his arm over the horse's back. "They seem to have taken a liking to you as well." He grinned as she stepped closer, her hand trailing over the destrier's neck.

"Angus seems to have taken a liking to your mother's cooking," she teased. "He has eaten nearly a dozen eggs and a rasher of bacon, all on his own." She laughed.

"My mother enjoys the challenge, or have you not noticed?" He licked his lips as she gazed up at him. Alexander held his breath. If she touched him, he might explode. His heart thundered in his chest.

"I have noticed a lot of things," she murmured, moving her hand to trail up his arm. Her touch sent awareness tingling and singing through his body. The folds of her dress mingled with the plaid draped around his waist. "Like how your body tenses when I touch you." Her hand slid into the fabric lying across his shoulder and traced it down, her thumb brushing over his brooch.

Alexander bit his lip. When her palm pressed flat against his chest, he groaned. Before she tempted him beyond reason, he needed to tell her.

"Madeline," he began, his voice hoarse. He cleared his throat, his hand closing over hers as it rested on his chest. "There is something I must ask you."

Her lashes fluttered as she met his gaze. He swallowed the lump rising in his throat, half fear, half hope. If he did not say it now, he probably would not get a better opportunity.

He led her from the pasture and down a small rolling hill overlooking a stream. Madeline stopped and picked a blue wildflower. The breeze caught a lock of her hair, carrying it across her face. He reached out and tucked it behind her ear. She smiled up at him, and he knew, beyond certainty, he would never be whole if she was not by his side.

"Marry me, lass," he whispered, cradling her chin in his hand. "I cannot live without you. Be my wife, my partner, and I promise to cherish you for the rest of your days."

Her lips parted, a breath escaping, but no words. He searched her eyes, his fingertips stroking the soft line of her jaw.

"What about my father?" she finally asked.

"Do you want to be with me?"

"Aye, more than I have ever wanted anything in my life," she replied, wrapping her arms around his waist.

He sighed against her hair as he embraced her. "Your father gave me permission to marry you. There is no reason to be concerned about that."

"How did he...It took you long enough to ask me, you daft..." Her words were lost when his lips collided with hers. She arched against him, her hands twisting in the fabric at his waist. She tasted of honey and sunshine. He delved between her lips, drinking from her sweetness. He wanted her for so long, and now he had her in his arms with the promise she would be his wife. Nothing could have made the moment richer.

A loud rouse of cheers rose up behind them. Alexander broke the kiss, leaning his forehead against hers. "Seems as though we have been discovered."

She pressed a soft kiss to his lips, a promise for later. "Save those thoughts for later, my handsome knight."

They turned to see his mother with his sisters standing beside Angus who held Heather high on his shoulders. Every one of them wore grins. His mother had her hands clasped before her, her eyes bright with tears. He could not help but embrace the joy in his heart. *This day is one of the best days of my life.*

He clasped Madeline's hand in his own and walked toward their family, overwhelmed with pride.

Chapter Nineteen

The sun hung low in the sky. Mary and Ruth fussed over Madeline until she pushed their hands away.

"Och, you are so lovely, Maddy," Ruth said, her rounded cheeks pink with excitement.

"Aye, like an angel," Mary added as she smoothed the back of Madeline's dress one last time.

With a deep breath and a nod, Madeline gestured toward the door. The girls hurried down the hall and outside. Madeline took her time, taking several deep breaths to calm herself. Finally, the day she had been waiting for. Part of her wished Evelyn could have been present for such a momentous occasion, but they could celebrate once she returned to her uncle's barony. She pressed her hand to her stomach and then walked out into the setting sun.

As she climbed the hill, Madeline spotted Angus and Alexander first. Her betrothed stood tall and proud, a smile playing on his lips. The grin on her brother's face betrayed his pride and joy. Off to the side stood Bonnie, Heather, Ruth, and Mary. All the attention focused on her as she came closer. Her heart swelled. It was truly one of the best days of her life.

Bonnie dabbed a kerchief at the corner of her eyes. Heather bounced from foot to foot, barely able to contain her excitement. His sisters looked on silently, their arms linked together, grinning at her.

Alexander stood tall and dashing against the afternoon sun. His damp hair slicked back away from his face. The clean plaid wrapped around him with care. Her handsome knight stole her breath away. She stopped next to him, and he gathered her hands in his. His eyes caught the sunset, their icy depths shattering into a deep blue warming her to the core. Soon he would be hers, forever.

Angus cleared his throat. He held a strip of ribbon and held their hands in his. As he wrapped the cloth around her hand and Alexander's, he spoke.

"Alexander and Madeline, as you stand here, I bind your hands together with this cloth, symbolizing the union of your lives and spirits in love and trust. Like the stars above you, your love should be a beacon of light, and like the earth beneath your feet, a firm foundation from which to grow. Be true to yourselves, to each other, and may you be blessed in your union from this day forward."

Angus wrapped the ribbon around their hands as he said the words, tying the ends together in a bow.

Madeline beamed up at Alexander, the joy threatening to burst from her in torrents of tears. He squeezed her hand.

"You may kiss your bride," Angus said as he stepped back.

Alexander drew her closer, sliding his free hand into her hair. She closed her eyes as he kissed her, savoring the warmth of the dying sunlight and the love emanating from him.

Cheers erupted around them. Madeline could not stop smiling. Finally, Alexander was her husband.

As the women embraced her, she could not help but think about that night. A flutter of excitement bubbled up inside her chest. Alexander belonged to her, to do with as she pleased. She met his gaze and sent him a smoldering glance filled with promises she intended to keep. This would be her first true taste of the passion she knew Alexander hid deep in his soul. Her wicked grin caught him unawares, and he arched a brow at her as they walked toward the house.

Later after the revelry, Madeline slipped into her chamber, exhausted. She placed the candle on the nightstand. She then pulled the flowers and pins from her hair, shaking it to fall in waves down her back. The door clicked shut behind her. She turned to see Alexander leaning against it. His broad frame nearly hid the door. His gaze raked over her loose hair, coming to rest on her face.

"You look as though you are starving," she quipped. "Did you not eat enough?"

He took a step toward her. "'Tis not food I crave at the

moment." His voice deepened with every word. A shiver of anticipation raced over her skin.

"Is there anything I can do for you, my lord?" she asked, batting her lashes innocently.

Alexander sucked in a breath. He reached for her. In a moment, she was pressed against him, her hands feeling the beating of his heart and the heat of his body.

"I have waited for this moment for years," he murmured, desire seeping into his tone.

"Why did you wait so long?" She wrapped her arms around his neck.

"The only way I would have you in my bed was if you were my wife." His statement startled her with its direct nature. "If I had a taste of you, I knew naught else would satisfy me. I needed all of you."

"I am yours now." She tangled her finger in a stray curl lying against his neck. "Take of me what you desire."

Alexander's hands wandered down her sides, grasping her hips. She sucked in a breath.

"I do not know where to start," he murmured. "It still feels like a dream, having you in my arms like this."

A fleeting wicked impulse forced Madeline to move her hands to where the plaid fastened at his waist. She slid it from its moorings and unwrapped it from his shoulders. Slowly her fingers pulled his shirt up and over his head. He said nothing but moved as she guided him to aid her quest.

She had seen Alexander's bare chest before, when he sparred with the other knights. But the excitement coursing through her now far outshone any delight she had at the sight of his body. The firelight played off his torso. She absently traced the indentations across his stomach. He groaned beneath her touch. It emboldened her. With a wicked grin, she trailed down, sliding her hand into the plaid wrapped around his waist. It loosened and dropped lower, the fabric now hanging precariously on his hips.

"Madeline," he said his voice low and strangled.

Her fingers wrapped around his manhood and he jerked,

taking a step back. The movement pulled him from her grasp and sent the plaid to the floor in a heap around his ankles. Her gaze honed in on his shaft, nestled in a thatch of dark hair. Her hands itched to touch him again. She wondered how he could be so hard and soft. Her curious nature begged for answers, but her body screamed for him to touch her again.

Madeline turned her back to him. "Would you help me with my laces?" She heard him move closer and held her breath as he pulled each lace loose. When he finished, she slid the dress down, revealing her shift. Her sensitive nipples brushed against the thin fabric. She shivered as she turned to face him.

He stood unmoving, his eyes dark and his lips pressed in a thin line. She gathered the hem in her hands and moved to pull it over her head, when he shifted, his hands coming to rest on her own.

"Let me," he whispered.

Madeline dropped her hands and held his gaze as he drew the shift up and off her, tossing it to the floor. Suddenly self-conscious, she moved to cover her breasts when he caught her wrists in his hands, his expression unreadable. He looked pained and uncertain. A deep furrow creased his brow. Perhaps he was displeased with what he saw. She hid her face behind a curtain of her hair.

"Do I displease you?" she murmured, fearing his reply.

A sudden shock of sensation hit her as his fingers brushed against the underside of her breasts. She arched against the touch as he dropped her wrists and cupped her breasts in his hands. His thumbs brushed across her nipples, and she gasped, meeting his gaze.

"Nay." He bent his head to kiss her again. His lips were warm and pliant. His hands wandered across her bare flesh, down to her hips. She squealed as his hand grabbed her backside, a palm on each cheek, and lifted her up.

He held her against him, her legs around his waist, her intimate place pressed to his stomach. The heat from his body set her aflame. She gripped his shoulders for balance.

Alexander moved to the bed and laid her down, then knelt

over her. One leg between her own, he hovered, barely touching her. He kissed her again, his tongue darting across her lips, begging for entrance. She welcomed him and deepened the kiss with a sigh, her hands tangling into his hair.

Madeline knew what happened between a man and a woman. She was no fool, but until this moment, she never imagined how much she would enjoy it. She savored the feel of his skin, the heat and the energy coiled inside the man.

His hand slid along the plane of her stomach, stopping just at her waist. Madeline broke the kiss when he hesitated. She searched his face.

"Mo chride." She kept her voice steady. "Touch me, I beg you." Madeline placed her hand on his and guided him to cup her aching mound. He sighed, burying his face in her neck and pressing kisses along the column of her throat.

His fingertips parted her sex and her legs fell open in invitation. He trailed a finger across her opening, and she moaned in response. As he stroked her, she grabbed at his shoulders, wanting him closer, wanting the feeling of skin against skin. When he slid a finger into her, she arched her head back, gasping for breath at the delicious invasion. She dug her fingernails into his flesh.

"Do you like when I touch you like this?" he murmured in her ear.

She nodded, her voice lost. He slid his finger in and out of her then added a second finger, stretching her. She bit her lip. He continued to caress her, feeding the hunger raging inside of her. But Madeline craved more. She bucked her hips against his hand. He chuckled and withdrew completely.

"What..." She tried to protest, but he kissed her again. Shifting his weight, he settled between her legs. While he teased her with his delicious kisses, he rubbed himself against her opening. When he slid inside, she froze, bracing her hands on his arms.

"Shhh..." he whispered against her lips. "It will only hurt for a moment, I promise."

Madeline nodded. He nuzzled against her neck, trailing

kisses along her neck and jaw, finally capturing her lips again.

He thrust into her, and she cried out in pain. Alexander held completely still. He lay fully sheathed inside her. Every part of her mind screamed he was too big, it would not work. He leaned his head against hers, whispering loving words in Gaelic. The pain began to ebb away, and she rocked her hips against his.

"Are you sure?" he asked softly.

Madeline nodded, kissing him. He moved inside of her, gently giving and taking. The motion showered sparks of pleasure over her. Soon she recognized the rhythm, and the sensations began to overtake her. Her body took control, meeting his thrusts with a tilt of her hips. He groaned against her mouth.

"Lass," he ground out, the kiss turning fierce and the thrusts increasing.

He slid his hand down between them. When he touched where they were joined, the pleasure exploded, taking hold of her. Her eyes snapped shut, her breaths turned to gasps. The starlight exploded behind her lids, every muscle in her body contracting, then slowly pulsing as her climax overwhelmed her.

Alexander increased his pace, his heavy breaths on her cheek as his body stiffened and he came inside of her, his warmth spilling into her. He rested his head against her own, his palm cradling her breast. She reached up and stroked a damp strand of hair away from his face.

"Are you well?" he asked. "Did I hurt you?"

"A pleasure worth the pain." She stroked his hair.

"It will not be that way again."

"I know." She smiled. They lay there for a few moments, basking in the warmth of their lovemaking.

Alexander stood. She sat up, her body tender in a delightful way. She glanced down, smears of blood on the inside of her thigh and on the blanket. He returned with a damp cloth and gently cleaned her. The tender gesture left her speechless. She lay back down as he finished. He cleaned himself and rejoined her on the bed, pulling her against his chest in a comforting embrace.

Madeline laid her head against him. His heartbeat created a

rhythmic lullaby. She grinned as her eyes drifted closed.

"I love you," she whispered against his skin. Sleep claimed her, and she never heard his reply.

Chapter Twenty

Alexander broke his fast early the next morning. His mother hovered over him, not saying much but smothering him with attention. He told her of his plans for them to leave that day. He saw the flicker of sadness cross her face, but she covered it with a smile.

"You do not have to leave yet," she said, putting more eggs on his plate. "You all need some rest."

"Aye, mother," he replied. "But we must return to the baron as quickly as possible. I must see how Gabriel fares as well."

His mother nodded as she sat down next to him. "I am proud of you." She reached out and stroked his hair. "Your father would be proud too, God rest his soul."

Alexander glanced at her. She sniffed a bit, blinking back tears. He captured her hand and held it between his own. "All will be well. You will see."

She nodded and squeezed his hand.

"Good morrow." Madeline stood behind them, having just risen herself. She looked lovely in a dark blue gown with red trimming and laces. Her hair was loosely braided and draped over one shoulder. His heart stopped at the sight of the angel he called his wife.

"Sit down, *m'eudail*." His mother stood and led Madeline to the seat beside Alexander. "Would you like some eggs? How about some bacon?"

"Nay, I thank you. I will take some porridge though if you have some made." Madeline sat down as his mother returned to the kitchen.

"Did you sleep well?" Alexander asked, watching her closely.

"Aye," she replied, a hint of blush creeping up into her cheeks. "Why did you not wake me?" She laid her hand on his thigh, giving it a gentle squeeze.

His eyes flew wide. "I thought you would wish to rest," he replied in a hushed tone.

Madeline pouted. "Next time, wake me. Then afterward we can rest together." She winked and trailed her hand higher, beneath his plaid.

Alexander gaped at her bold advances. It seems as though he had unleashed a sensual beast inside of her. The look she gave him from beneath her lashes made him harder than a loaf of week old bread.

"Madeline." He tried to sound stern, but it came out more like a groan. The tips of her fingers brushed against the head of his shaft. "You need to stop," he whispered and laid his hand over hers.

She pouted, her lower lip deliciously full and moist. The urge to kiss her nearly overtook his common sense. With a gentle squeeze, she removed her hand. Her gaze drifted to the doorway behind him.

"I thank you kindly," Madeline said as his mother approached, setting a bowl of porridge on the table before her.

Alexander cleared his throat, willing his body to relax. Her curious touch sent his mind into a whirl, every sensation intensified now. He needed to get some air. Standing, he nodded to his mother and Madeline then took his leave of them.

Their conversation picked up, and he heard the gentle music of Madeline's laughter as he stepped from the house.

The day proved to be perfect for traveling. Since the horses were rested and well fed, he anticipated them reaching the baron's keep within the next two days. Scar met him at the fence. He rubbed his hand along the stallion's neck, giving him a soft pat.

"We are leaving then?" The feminine voice interrupted his quiet musings. He turned to see Heather watching him with curious eyes.

"Aye," Alexander replied. "Why are you not in the house breaking your fast with the others?"

"I was running through the meadow with Mutt, hunting rabbits."

"Did you catch any?"

She shook her head. "Nay, Mutt is not very good at sneaking up on them." The large hairy dog came to her side and plopped down on his haunches, nuzzling her skirts. She patted him on the head. "Can I bring him with me?"

"I am afraid you cannot." Alexander knelt down to her level. He truly regretted not being able to bring the dog. They played well together, but the four of them needed to keep a low profile as they traveled. A dog would complicate their journey.

Heather pouted, but she nodded. The girl hesitated and then charged, slamming into him. Her good arm curved around his neck, and her face buried in the curve of it. She pulled back and bit her lip.

"What was that for?" he asked, stunned by her affection. His hands rested on her shoulders.

"For everything," she said, grinning. "You have given me a real true adventure. I have always dreamt of one." She pressed a tender kiss to his scruffy cheek.

"We are family now," he reminded her with a smile. "I would say treat me like you do one of your own brothers, but I have seen the way you treat them."

She blushed a bit. "I shall treat you better than them," Heather promised.

"Good." He stood and held her hand. "Care to help me with the horses then?"

Heather grinned as she followed him into the pasture. A sense of peace began to settle over him. Finally, everything was falling into place, as if it were meant to be.

The sun dropped low on the horizon. Madeline missed the comfort and companionship of Alexander's family. She sighed. Their departure had left a bitter taste in her mouth. She longed to spend time with her new family, although in her heart she knew they needed to be on their way.

Alexander had been quite solemn all day. She hoped it had not been anything she had done. Their first night together had been a culmination of the months of waiting and wanting. She allowed herself a secret smile, remembering his touch, his kiss. The heat rose in her cheeks. She fanned herself with her hand. Her husband was truly a magnificent lover, content to please her in ways she had never imagined.

It had also disappointed her to not wake in his arms. She had woken with a chill, reaching for him on the bed. Perhaps she had disappointed him somehow. Madeline worried her lower lip between her teeth. Was that why he pushed her away at the morning meal? Worry overwhelmed her. She forcefully shoved it aside as Heather rode up alongside her.

"Are you well, Maddy?" her little sister asked, cocking her head.

"Aye, my love," she replied. No reason to tell her sister her silly concerns. "How fares your arm?"

Heather raised her bandaged arm. "'Tis itching like mad and aches a bit, but Bonnie gave me some paste to take care that."

Madeline smiled lovingly at the young girl. It would do Heather well to be taught the proprieties and manners of a highborn lady. Not as if she could not have gotten the same teaching at her father's keep. Heather had been quite well behaved for most of the trip, keeping her comments to herself and behaving in a less boyish manner.

"When are we stopping for the night?" Heather asked. The sun had nearly set. She glanced at the orange and red sky darkening into a nighttime blue.

Madeline shrugged. "I am not sure. Perhaps Alexander knows of an inn ahead where we can rest."

Heather nodded, and the silence stretched between them as they continued to follow along behind. The sun disappeared, and the moon, just past full, peeked from behind a string of clouds. It had grown late when they finally reached a small village. Alexander halted at the inn.

Madeline had never been so relieved to get out of the saddle as she did at that moment. Her backside ached, and she surmised the fault lay somewhere other than sitting in a saddle all day. Her face heated at the memories. She would share his bed again tonight. The thought thrilled her.

"Angus, take the horses around to the stables. I will go in and secure us lodging for the night," Alexander said as he helped her down from the saddle.

His touch set her heart to racing. She allowed her hands to linger on his arms for a moment longer. Then he turned from her to help Heather down from her horse.

Madeline held Heather's hand and followed Alexander into the inn. They stood patiently off to the side as he spoke with the innkeeper. A dozen curious pairs of eyes turned toward them. Madeline pulled Heather closer to her side.

Alexander returned to her. "I have secured two rooms. One for you and Heather, the other I will share with Angus."

Madeline opened her mouth to protest the arrangements, then snapped it shut. He must be angry with her, to push her away like this. She nodded and walked past him. The innkeeper led her and Heather up the stairs. She had too much pride to glance over her shoulder and see if Alexander was watching.

Alexander was sitting at a table in the far corner of the room with a mug of ale in his hand when Angus joined him. Already on his third drink, his head started to feel a bit lighter than it normally did.

"You started drinking without me?" Angus shook his head and waved the barmaid over. "I will take a pint and a trencher of stew if you have it."

With a nod and a coy smile, she left them.

"How many have you had then?" Angus asked, leaning back in his chair and stretching his legs out.

"Three." Alexander did not even look at him. He was struggling to shake the image of Madeline's disappointment. He wanted to share her bed. Hell, he wanted to take her over and over again. Feel her lithe body wiggling underneath him as he made her fall apart with pleasure. He sighed and took another drink. She needed her rest as they all did. They had at least another day's journey until they reached the border.

"I have never seen you imbibe more than one in an evening." Angus watched him intently. "What has my sister done to you now? Or better still, what have you done to her?"

Alexander hesitated, unsure if he should explain his troubles to Angus. He sighed, the alcohol affecting him enough not to care one whit either way.

"I refused to share her bed tonight," Alexander confessed, finishing the ale in one long swallow.

Angus left out a long low whistle. "I cannot help you there. That is between the two of you."

The barmaid returned with two pitchers of ale and two trenchers. "Looks like you both could use some food." She turned and left them.

"Sweet little thing, she is," Angus commented on the barmaid as she sashayed to a table of men on the other side of the room. He took a bite of food and washed it down. "But I have sworn off women."

Alexander's lip twitched as he tried to suppress his laughter. It seemed as though Angus still fumed about the events with the woman in red a few days ago. She had seduced him, incapacitated him, and then stolen all his coin. All in all it was tragic but quite amusing at the same time. Then Alexander remembered his own situation. A vague memory of him scolding Gabriel over his infatuation and pursuit of Lady Evelyn resurfaced. Ah, aye, it had come back to haunt him. *Love truly does make fools of us all.* Perhaps he had been too hasty in pushing Madeline from his bed.

He ate the meal so generously provided for him. Pushing away the mug of ale, he ate several bites and found himself ravenous. The two men ate in silence and then sat in the common room. There were at least a dozen other men, all of them drinking.

"I believe I shall retire." Alexander stood up.

"I wish you would have gotten three rooms," Angus replied.

"We may be brothers, but I have no wish to share a bed with you." He laughed at his own joke.

He stood and joined Alexander, who swayed slightly on his feet. His tolerance for drink seemed to be worse than he had remembered. They stumbled up the stairs, unaware of the gazes following them.

Chapter Twenty-One

He stood in the darkness, his gaze scanning the hillsides. He and his men had lost their trail after the small village inn. There were towns scattered along the main road heading south, but they had scoured every one. He spat and folded his arms across his chest.

It made no sense to him how they could just vanish. They had kept off the main road. He shook his head. There could be no way they knew he was tracking them. He had hoped to ambush them in the forests. But they had evaded him thus far. Likely they sought shelter with a friend or relative. He remembered Alexander mentioning his clan hailed from this area of the lowlands. They would place some delicate inquiries in the morn.

The door swung open behind him, heavy footsteps stopped short of where he stood. He turned slightly.

"What do you want?" he asked, a thin hint of irritation in his voice.

"They are here," the man said.

He uncrossed his arms and turned toward Malcom. "Are you sure 'tis them?"

"Aye," Malcom replied. "They are already abed."

"You did not think to fetch me as soon as they arrived," he snapped. Then a thought calmed him. "Perhaps this is in my favor. Have you heard details of their destination?"

Malcolm shook his head.

He stroked his chin. "I shall have to speak with the innkeeper." He considered the different directions he could take his plot. "Did they recognize you or any of the other men?"

"Nay." Malcom rubbed the back of his neck. "We kept our heads in our cups for the most part. They showed no indication they had recognized us."

"Good." He walked toward the door. "Tell the men to rest,

we will rise before the sun." He did not even wait for a reply. Inside the door, he veered off to the kitchens and cornered the innkeeper as he counted his coin.

"Can I help you, sir?" The balding old man looked up from his purse. He tightened the strings and tucked the little bag into his pocket.

"I heard you have new guests this night," he began cautiously. "Any chance you know where they are headed?" He leaned against the table.

"Aye, two lovely lasses and their escorts. They are making their way to the border." The old man grinned, showing a smattering of dark spaces where his teeth used to be.

"How far is the border from here?" he asked, the information churning in his mind.

"About a day's ride if you follow the road." The old man scratched his beard. "Leads right into a thick patch of forest before you reach the English lands."

"I thank you kindly." He laid two coins on the table. "I would rather you not mention this conversation to anyone, it would be greatly appreciated."

The old man's eyes lit up. "Do not worry none on that count, sir."

He turned and left the inn by the same door he had entered moments before. They were headed for the border. A vague memory nagged at the back of his mind. He remembered talking to Madeline's brother, Rodric. They had both been drinking quite heavily. Rodric had mentioned Madeline spent the last ten years as the ward of an English baron. It had surprised him the laird would allow her to live with the *sassenach*. But the baron was her uncle. If he could remember the name of the barony...It started with an *R. Rayne*. That was it. *The Baron of Rayne*.

He would stake all the coin in his pocket they were headed there. A wicked grin split his lips. Glancing heavenward, he admired the clear night. On the morrow, they would have to take them. The forest would make the perfect cover for an ambush. He would send half his men ahead tonight, and the rest would follow after their quarry left in the morning.

Finally, she would be his, as well as her dowry and her father's complete compliance with his demands. The laughter bubbling from his lips held no humor, only fiendish delight.

Madeline grew concerned when she and Heather were the first ones dressed and waiting in the common room. She frowned. It was already well past dawn, and she had hoped to make it to the barony as soon as possible. They were so close. She wanted to see Evelyn desperately, to tell her everything that had happened.

Heather sat next to her eating a bowl of porridge, completely oblivious to anything around her.

"Wait here. I shall return in a moment." Madeline crossed the common room and ascended the stairs. Her brother and husband shared the room next to hers. She poised to knock on the door. Steeling herself against her sudden bout of nerves, she rapped on the wood, softly at first, then a bit louder. No answer. She frowned. Trying the handle, she pushed it open without any force.

Alexander lay sprawled across the bed, stomach down, his hair mussed and covering his eyes. Angus was lying on the floor, a blanket beneath his head. He seemed uncomfortable. She felt guilty they had to share a room, but then remembered it had been at Alexander's insistence they do so. Madeline pushed the guilt away.

She walked over to Angus and nudged him with her foot. He grunted and waved a hand at her but never opened his eyes. She kicked him again, a bit harder in the ribs.

"What in the bloody hell..." His eyes shot open and his gaze darted around the room. Angus struggled to pull his dagger out, until he spotted her. He slumped back against the blanket again. "Saints alive, Maddy. That is no way to wake a man."

Madeline crossed her arms, her foot tapped impatiently. "'Tis well past dawn. Both of you slothful louts need to get a move on if we are to make it to the baron's keep before dark."

"Och, God's teeth." Angus groaned as he stood. He snatched his sword and his saddle bag. "I shall meet you outside." He pushed past her to head down to the common room.

"Heather is breaking her fast in the main room. Be sure she stays out of trouble." Madeline saw him nod as he disappeared out the door. She wondered if he had drunk too much the night before. It always seemed to make men quite lethargic the following morning. She had noticed far too much of that type of behavior at the tournament and all the tourneys she had ever attended.

Madeline turned to the bed. Her gaze lingered on her husband's calf and followed it up over the curve of his hip and buttocks, across his broad back, and stopped at his shaggy head. She tutted her disapproval and sat down on the bed next to him. With a gentle hand, she pressed against his shoulder, shaking him slightly.

"Alexander," she murmured, hoping to wake him gently. He merely grunted and turned away from her. She frowned and shook him harder. "Wake up." He did nothing.

Glancing around the room, she spied a pitcher of water on the nightstand. She stood and picked up the pitcher. Madeline raised it over his head and poured the contents over his sleeping form.

Alexander swore and shifted restlessly on the bed, grumbling as he sat up. He glared in her direction. His hair soaking wet and matted to his head in thick patches. She giggled at the sight. He looked like a drowned rat.

"That was uncalled for, wife." He ran his hand through his hair, pushing it back away from his eyes. His cool stare rested on her as he stood. "You are angry with me."

"Aye," she said, placing the pitcher back on the stand and propping her hands on her hips.

"I..." He let the words trail off and shrugged.

"Did you drink too much ale last eve?" she asked, eyeing him closely. If he did drink too much, he had only himself to blame. Madeline knew him to be a man of moderate tastes, but she had seen the look on his face before she left him the prior evening. He had appeared half ready to kill someone and the other half ready to drown in a cask of ale.

Alexander shook his head. The motion made him pause, and he clasped his head in both hands.

"Are you even able to ride?" she asked him, stepping a bit closer.

"I shall survive this, too. I am sure," he replied but made no movement to stand.

"Is there anything I can get for you?" Madeline hated to see him suffering, even if she was still sore at him. He had brought it all upon himself. Unable to resist, she reached out and stroked the top of his head. The wet strands of hair slipping beneath her fingertips.

He reached up and gently pulled her down to sit across his lap. Alexander leaned his head against hers, pressing a kiss to her cheek.

"You are not upset with me?" she murmured, enjoying the softness of his lips against her jaw. He nibbled on the lobe of her ear. Her eyes drifted closed.

"Should I be angry with you?" His words caressed the delicate shell of her ear. A delightful shiver trickled through her body. "Have you done something wrong?" His hand grasped her breast over the material of her dress.

Madeline wished he was touching her overheated skin. Being so close to him made her body react. Her breaths came in pants, her body wept for his touch. She wiggled on his lap.

Alexander groaned, his hand squeezing her breast harder. "If you continue, my love, we will never be able to leave this room. At least not until I taste you again." His kiss trailed over the skin of her neck. The sensations assaulted her, burning her from the inside out. She tilted her head back, allowing him access to continue his explorative kisses.

"I assumed I did something wrong," she confessed. "The other night." Madeline turned to meet his gaze when she felt the heat of his lips leave her skin cold and bereft.

"Wrong?" He seemed puzzled. "Why would you think you did something wrong?" He grasped her chin when she turned away embarrassed. "You are perfect, in every way."

"I just thought..." She trailed off, shrugging her shoulders.

"You thought what?" His gaze warmed her to the core. She could see the concern in his eyes.

"You were gone."

He stared at her, confusion stirring across his features.

"The morning after you made love to me," she murmured. "I woke, and you were gone."

Alexander shook his head. "Love," he replied stroking her hair back. "I wanted to wake you. Just seeing you naked and lying there asleep was enough to rouse me to passion. But you needed to rest. Climbing into the saddle would be painful enough without my adding to your discomfort."

She blushed at the memory. Her body had been sore from the arduous journey they made so far, and he, having taken her maidenhead, had caused her additional strain and aches. But she craved his touch desperately, even now. "Is this why you refused to share a room with me last eve?"

"Aye," he whispered against her skin as he kissed along her jaw. The contact drove any residual anger from her mind, replacing it with lust.

"I understand your concern, but the desire to have you inside me again drives all fear of pain away." She licked her lips and threaded her fingers in his hair. "Now that I have had you, I refuse to be denied. I will take what is mine." She kissed him again with a fierce passion sinking into her very core. He pulled her closer, crushing her against his chest.

A soft knock interrupted their torrid embrace. Madeline broke the kiss and leaned her head against Alexander's. Their panting breaths tangled together. She fought for control of herself again.

"The horses are ready," Angus said from the doorway. She heard the sound of his boots clicking on the floor as they receded down the hall.

"God's blood, can I never find a moment alone with you?"

She grumbled, frustration lacing her voice.

Alexander chuckled. "When we reach the baron's keep, I am sure he will give us some much deserved time alone."

"He had better." She smiled coyly at him. "I have a few things I would like to try."

He arched his brow in question. "What kind of things?"

"I want to know what your cock tastes like," she whispered, pressing her hand to his groin and squeezing him.

"Madeline!" He stared at her in shock. "Where did you hear such language?"

"There is much you do not know about me, *mo chride*." She slid off his lap, disappointed at the sudden loss of his warmth. They had to leave, wasting any more time would delay their arrival, and Madeline was anxious to reach the keep. She missed her cousin and her uncle, but what she truly desired happened to be the man watching her with a wicked smirk on his lips.

"I had no doubts you were a vixen." He slipped behind her, wrapping his arm around her waist and pressing a kiss to her head. "Let us go, before Angus decides to return threatening force if we do not hurry."

She giggled and led the way down to the common room and out the front door. Angus and Heather were already mounted. Alexander helped Madeline into the saddle. As she gathered her reins, she wheeled the horse around and spurred it into motion. This day she decided she would take the lead.

Chapter Twenty-Two

The afternoon wore on as their small group entered the forest. They had made good time. Alexander was beginning to see more familiar territory. He allowed Madeline to lead them for most of the day, but, as they approached the shaded woods, he reclaimed the lead in case bandits decided to attack them. If all went well, they could make it to the baron's keep not long after nightfall.

Alexander listened to Angus' boisterous tale of a monk and a cardinal meeting for drinks in a tavern. He shook his head. Having to deal with both Angus and Gabriel would prove to be an interesting adventure. He prayed his brother had healed. Many nights he wondered about Gabriel's fate, whether he was still sick with fever or dead. He hoped Evelyn's ministrations aided in his recovery and granted him a desire to survive. They deserved every happiness. He glanced back at Madeline. *As does she*. He wanted to provide her with her heart's desires.

He never saw the arrow as it whistled toward him until it slammed into his left shoulder. Alexander spun in reflex, the pain searing through his flesh and down his arm. His horse slowed to a standstill as he writhed in the saddle, gripping the pommel with his uninjured arm.

Angus moved to his side in an instant. The agony burned as he focused his attention on the direction of the shot. His vision blurred as a group of figures materialized from the forest ahead of them.

"Angus," he grunted. "Help me down and hand me my sword."

Without another word, Angus slid off his horse, catching him as he struggled to step down from the saddle.

The figures approached slowly. He felt the hilt of his sword slide into his palm. The ache throbbed with every movement, but he had to fight. Madeline and Heather needed him. Angus could not hold them off himself. He shoved the pain aside and glanced up at the oncoming men.

"How many can you see?" he asked Angus, shaking his head to free the cobwebs of agony from taking hold.

"Seven," Angus said.

"Are the women still on horseback?"

"Aye."

"On my mark—" Alexander swallowed "—tell them to ride like the devil is on their heels." He barely caught Angus' nod. "Let us give these bastards a fight they will not soon forget."

With a yell, Alexander charged forward, his sword raised. He heard Angus shout to his sisters. His vision cleared as his sword made contact with the first man's. He allowed the rage to flood him, the memories of his brother lying at his feet in a pool of blood fueling his ire. The pain ebbed into the background as he parried against the man. He spun away from the swing of his opponent's blade, catching him off guard. He drove his sword into the man's side. He dropped like a stone, and Alexander turned to the next man.

"Enough!" The shout caught him off guard. "I believe you have something which belongs to me."

Alexander turned in the direction of the voice.

A figure emerged from the shadows. *McLairn.*

"I do not have anything belonging to you," Alexander spat, flinching as he jerked his shoulder back.

McLairn focused his attention on Alexander's wound. A sadistic grin twisted his lips. "I hope you like my welcoming gift," he said, gesturing to the arrow protruding from Alexander's shoulder.

"Go to hell." Alexander would not give him the satisfaction of seeing him in pain. He pushed it back and stood up straight.

"I do not think you are in any position to be giving orders, *Sassenach.*"

Alexander betrayed no emotion. Only Angus, Madeline, and the laird knew he was English. He gritted his teeth, biting back a response. A quick glance over his shoulder showed Madeline and Heather had fled. A wave of relief washed over him. Angus sank to his knees, a sword at his throat. He met his gaze and nodded. Alexander turned his attention back to McLairn.

"What made you think you could march your dirty arse into my land and take what belonged to me?" McLairn glared at him, the hatred and pride marring his perfect features.

"Madeline never belonged to you." Alexander practically growled.

"Ah, but there is where you are wrong." The man stepped closer, his hand resting on the hilt of his sword. "Madeline belonged to me long before she ever left the highlands, pledged when she was but a child."

Alexander bit his lip. Why had the laird not mentioned any of this before he had whisked Madeline away and made her his wife. He wanted to feel regret for breaking a promised betrothal, but he could not muster the indignation. McLairn was not fit to clean her chamber pot. Alexander held his head high.

"Then why did Laird Campbell offer her hand to the winner of the tournament and not follow through on his contract with your family?" Alexander asked.

"'Tis none of your bloody business, English," McLairn snapped, stepping even closer and pulling his blade from its sheath. "Madeline Campbell is mine and so is her worth."

Alexander recognized the strategy; he had seen it many times before. McLairn wanted the money and influence that came with being married to the Campbell clan. He was dangerous, drunk on the delusion he was entitled to what had been promised all those years ago.

"'Tis not my fault my brothers decided to start stealing from the Campbell's lands, taking what is owed us." He shrugged. "It was to be ours after the marriage anyway."

"You were reaping the bounty of her dowry before you claimed your bride?" Alexander grimaced at the affront. Little wonder Laird Campbell decided to withdrawal from the betrothal.

"It was mine by rights!" McLairn screamed and pointed the sword at Alexander's chest.

The thundering of hooves distracted Alexander for a

moment. McLairn dropped his sword as he turned toward the approaching horses. Alexander's heart dropped into his stomach when he saw the riders. Four of them approached. The first two held women before the riders in the saddle who held daggers to their throats. *Madeline and Heather.* Alexander stepped forward to go to them when McLairn's voice stopped him.

"One move and they die."

The icy fingers of dread trailed over Alexander's heart. "You are bluffing." He met the madman's gaze.

"Am I?" His grin glinted, predatory and wild. "Both daughters of the laird. Both of value to me. But I only need one." He tapped his chin with a slender finger. "Which one will it be? Go ahead. Test me."

Alexander tossed his sword to the ground. The sword his father gave him before he passed. A sword he had never surrendered before and now only did so with reluctance. But he refused to gamble with their lives and heaved a sigh as McLairn's remaining men encircled him and Angus, tying their hands behind their backs. He wanted to scream as they twisted his injured shoulder to tie his hands. But he bit his lip. The taste of blood flooded his mouth.

He hung his head as they led them into the forest, well away from the main road. Alexander watched from the corner of his eye, making sure Madeline and Heather remained unharmed. He struggled to block out the pain from his injury and formulate a plan. But at the moment, it seemed as though his luck had finally run out.

Madeline glared at McLairn as they entered the small encampment. Her worried gaze kept returning to Alexander. He dragged his feet as he walked, his head bobbing even though he tried to keep it steady. His side was soaked with blood from the wound in his shoulder. She needed to tend to him.

They bound Heather as they did Alexander and Angus and

shoved them down against a large tree. Alexander collapsed, his head falling back against the tree. Angus' lips were pressed together in a thin line. Heather's face was streaked with tears. Her broken arm twisted behind her. She hiccupped a soft sob but kept her chin up in pure defiance. Madeline jerked her hands away when they grabbed her.

"McLairn!" she shouted. "Let me take care of his wound at least."

The man she had come to know as quiet and pensive had transformed into a devil. He turned toward her, a wicked gleam in his dark eyes.

"Why would I let you do that?" he asked, his voice sliding over her like snail slime.

"At least let me remove the arrow." Madeline cringed as he approached her, but she stood her ground.

Pushing past her, he knelt down beside Alexander and cocked his head. Before she could react, McLairn ripped the arrow out of Alexander's shoulder. His scream echoed through the trees, and he slumped over, unconscious. McLairn stood and walked away, tossing the arrow onto the ground.

Madeline rushed past him and dropped to her knees, cradling Alexander's head in her hands. His skin faded to a pale hue, and his clothes were soaked in sweat and blood.

When one of the men grabbed at her, she grabbed hold of his hand and bent his finger back. He grabbed her braid and jerked her head back, knocking her to the ground.

"Leave her be." McLairn gave a dismissive flick of his wrist. The man grumbled, clutching his injured fingers as he walked away.

Madeline scrambled to her knees again. "Alexander," she said trying to wake him. "Can you hear me?" He just lay there in a heap against the tree. She glanced at Angus for guidance.

"You are going to have to stop the bleeding, lass." Her brother's face betrayed his concern and anger, but he walked her through the process. She wished she had gone with Evelyn to see Old Nora and learn the secrets of healing. But it was not a moment for regrets, so she pushed them away.

Madeline gently peeled back the fabric of his plaid and shirt. The blood had darkened the cream fabric of his shirt to a wine red. She swallowed hard and ripped his shirt, just over the wound. A jagged hole marred his strong shoulder. She ripped part of her own skirt and dabbed wound, trying to clean it. Glancing around, she spotted one of the men drinking from a leather flagon.

"Give me that," she ordered, pointing to him. The man sighed and glanced at his leader, who was busy speaking with two other men. He hesitated for a moment and then tossed it to her. She caught it and quickly poured the contents over Alexander's wound. It held whisky, not water. She cursed, hoping she had not just made things worse. Alexander jerked at the contact of the alcohol on his wound but did not wake.

Madeline ripped his shirt off his shoulder, hoping to get access to the wound on his back. She poured the liquid over the wound. He arched his back and groaned. She dabbed the area, wiping away the blood. A fresh stream of blood trickled from the wound.

"Rip some of the cloth and press it over the wound; smooth the edges of the wound first." Angus instructed. "The bastard should not have ripped the arrow out as he did."

"Will it heal?" Madeline asked, concern furrowing her brow as she worked at bandaging the wound on his back.

Angus shook his head. "I do not know, but if the bleeding does not stop, he will not last long enough to find out."

Madeline whispered a quick prayer, and then focused her attention on the wound in the front. She cleaned it the best she could, pushing the torn skin flat where possible, and stuck a small wad of clean rag into the hole. She pressed her hand against the wad of cloth. Alexander remained pale, a sheen of sweat on his brow, his breathing labored and shallow. Madeline prayed harder than she ever had before. Looking at Heather's sling, she got an idea to a bandage the wound to hold everything in place. She tore more linen strips from Alexander's shirt.

She scanned the group of men. They milled around a small fire in the middle of the camp. Once the bandages were secured,

Madeline leaned her head against Alexander's chest.

What will I do now? She searched the camp. McLairn had disappeared. She breathed a sigh of relief. At least she did not have to face him, but she knew at some point he would return for her. Her mind raced. They were not far from the barony. The border lay just beyond the ridge. If they could get free, they could make it. But with Alexander unconscious and no way to rouse him, they were at McLairn's mercy.

"Rest, Maddy," Angus whispered, as if sensing her distress. "I have a plan."

Madeline nodded and closed her eyes, comforted by the rhythm of his breaths mingling with the gentle pulse of his heart. Within moments, she fell asleep.

As the men drank, Angus feigned sleep. But he remained wide awake, keeping close measure of the men in the camp. They were drunk on whisky. He counted nine men. McLairn had returned, now asleep in the corner of the camp. Another man stood a few feet away, his eyes fixed squarely on Madeline who slumbered against Alexander.

Angus grew concerned. Alexander still had not woken from McLairn's torturous assault earlier. Madeline had done her best to clean the wounds, but if they did not reach a healer soon, Angus feared the wound would fester. He tugged gently on his bonds. They were tight. Heather snored softly beside him, her head on his arm. He had never been more proud of her than at this moment. Her strength would help them.

A boisterous round of laughter rocked the group of men around the campfire. Their stoic guard moved closer to the fire to hear the commotion. He turned his head away, half listening to the conversation of his companions and half watching the prisoners.

Carefully sliding his hands against Heather's side, he felt the tiny dagger tucked into her small bodice. They never would have thought to check the wee lass for a weapon. They were fortunate she never had the chance to use it on them. A grin cracked his lips. Those bastards would have begged for mercy from a wee slip of a girl. He had taught Heather how to use it, so he knew her to be well-equipped and prepared to draw blood.

He twisted the dagger in his hands and sliced through the bonds with a gentle motion as not to arouse suspicion. He kept his eyes closed, and his breaths measured. Focusing on the task at hand, he cut the rope and the restraints loosened.

After a few minutes, they fell away. He continued the charade, waiting for the opportune moment. He rested there, aware of every sound, every movement around him. Once the men passed out, he would make his move, take out the guard, and they would be away from the camp quickly. He just prayed Alexander would wake.

Chapter Twenty-Three

His head pounded and his shoulder burned like the fires of hell. Alexander wrenched his eyes open with a groan.

"Shhh," a soft whisper hushed him.

Alexander glanced to his left. Angus sat beside him, his eyes wide as he nodded toward the sleeping men. The pain overwhelmed him, and Alexander felt nauseated. He pushed it all back into a hidden part of his mind. The pain, the nausea, the fire beneath his skin. He realized McLairn's men were asleep.

Angus pulled his hands from behind his back, showing his freed wrists. Alexander nodded and shifted forward as Angus cut his bonds. Madeline stirred against him. He had not even noticed her weight leaning against him. Her hands were covered in blood. He glanced at his shoulder. She had cleaned his wound, but it needed more attention than her basic care.

Angus moved on to wake and free Heather. Alexander stroked Madeline's cheek. Her eyes fluttered open, and he pressed his fingertips to her lips. She nodded as she rose from his lap quietly. Angus stood and helped Alexander to his feet.

Agony tore through his shoulder. He bit his lip to keep from crying out. A whimper escaped him. They moved quietly as a group to where the horses were tethered. They carefully slipped them away from the camp, while keeping a watchful eye on the sleeping captors.

Alexander leaned against a tree, taking a deep breath. Then he remembered. *My sword.* He could not leave without his father's sword. He knew it was ridiculous to risk capture over a weapon, but it held too much value to him to leave in the hands of cutthroats. The others had already mounted and were waiting for him.

"Go," he said softly, "I shall be right behind you."

Madeline hesitated for a moment but finally nudged her

horse to follow the others. Alexander crept back into the camp, aware of every breath, every sound. He neared the place where McLairn slept, and he saw his sword, leaning against the base of the tree.

He reached out for it, careful not to make any sudden movements or sounds. As his fingers grasped around the hilt, he drew it toward him. Clutching it to his chest, he turned to leave them behind. Alexander stumbled, weak from the injury, and slammed into the nearest tree, reinjuring his shoulder. He yelped from the agonizing pain screaming through his body.

In an instant, they surrounded him, swords drawn and at his throat. McLairn eyed him, and then glanced at the spot where they had been tied.

"They have escaped," he shouted. "Find them." Half of the men jumped at his order, swinging onto horseback and riding toward the border. McLairn sneered at Alexander. "You will pay, *Sassenach*. You will pay dearly."

Alexander felt the blow hit him in the back of the head. *At least she escaped.* His last thoughts as he crumpled to the ground and the darkness embraced him.

A frigid splash of water doused his face and body, waking him. Alexander shook his head, plastering his wet hair to his scalp. The water ran down his face and soaked his clothing. He wrenched his eyes open and glared at the man holding the bucket.

McLairn tossed the empty container to the ground. "Glad to see you have not died yet, *Sassenach*."

Alexander leaned back against the tree. The sun was setting. He had been unconscious all day. *Damn.* His hands were bound together in his lap. The ache and burn in his left shoulder warned him of the possibility of infection.

Weakness threatened to consume him, but he held McLairn's gaze, forcing every ounce of strength into his stoic expression. He refused to give the bloody bastard the satisfaction of defeating him. The thought of Madeline, Heather, and Angus reaching the baron's keep without incident gave him hope. Licking his lips, he winced as his tongue slid across a cut.

"You have lost, McLairn," Alexander muttered, keeping his gaze steady on the arrogant man before him. "Go home with your tail tucked between your legs."

An amused chuckle burst from McLairn. "You are in no position to negotiate, *Sassenach*." A woman's scream echoed through the trees.

Alexander's eyes darted in the direction of the cry. He forced himself to be passive, to not show any emotion, but his heart thundered in his chest. The fear clenched his insides, tearing at his soul. *Nay, it could not be. Please, God.*

"I will have your lovely woman. Then I shall let my men take her, one by one, until she is a mere shell of what she once was." McLairn's lips curled back in a sickening grin. "'Tis you who has lost."

Another shrill cry echoed in the dim forest. Alexander hung his head, refocusing his energy into formulating a plan. To McLairn, the action symbolized defeat. Internalizing all the pain, Alexander shoved it into his anger and fueled it. He waited until McLairn turned and walked away to begin working on the bonds at his wrists. Wiggling them, he knew he would never be able to break free without a blade. He closed his eyes and prayed they had not searched him before binding his hands. As he slid his hand down the inside of his boot, he whispered a prayer to the saints. The cool steel comforted him as he slipped it into his palm. He relaxed his body as he concentrated on cutting the rope.

Another scream pierced the darkening forest. His head snapped up. *Stay strong, Madeline.* He worked faster, careful not to draw attention to himself. Alexander prayed he would not be too late.

Chapter Twenty-Four

Madeline raced through the woods following Angus and Heather as their horses charged through the darkness. The moon was beginning to wane, but more than enough moonlight shone to guide them down the road. When they reached the village, Madeline knew they were close. She glanced over her shoulder. No one followed behind them.

"Whoa," she said, reining the horse to a walk. Angus heard her slow and gestured for Heather to walk as well. He brought his horse beside hers and they rode silently past the village.

"How far?" Angus asked his voice low.

"Not far now." Madeline searched the horizon. The darkness was breaking into a lighter shade of blue signaling the approaching dawn. She turned in the saddle again, hoping to catch sight of Alexander. Her heart sank. What if he had been recaptured? She swallowed the lump in her throat.

They continued down the road in silence as the sun rose. The sunlight streamed through the trees, casting early morning shadows on them. As they rode, Madeline kept her head down, her heart heavy with worry.

"Look!" Heather excited statement broke the sullen silence.

Madeline glanced up, catching a glimpse of the stone walls rising through the tree line. They urged their mounts into a trot as they approached the gates.

"I have come to see my uncle," she called out as the guards stepped into their path. "I am Lady Madeline Campbell. Let me pass."

"'Tis she. You may enter, my lady," the taller guard said, recognizing her.

"I thank you, good sir." Madeline led the way into the inner bailey. She slid from the horse's back and faced the familiar stone building. Taking a deep breath, she strode toward the great hall. A flicker of movement from the corner of her eye caught her attention. Turning toward it, her jaw fell open.

Alexander limped toward her, a smile on his lips. She ran toward him, wrapping her arms around him. He winced as she slammed into him, holding his side.

"Madeline…" he began, but she silenced him as she grabbed a hold of his face and pressed her lips to his. He stiffened against her. Pushing against her shoulders, he backed away. "Maddy…" His voice was drowned out by another.

"Why are you kissing my husband?"

Her eyes wide, she glanced to her left. Evelyn stood with her hand on her hip, her jaw thrust out, foot tapping impatiently.

"Husband?" Madeline squeaked, her gaze returning to the man before her. "Alexander, what…?" Her heart sank into the pit of her stomach, and she felt the bile rise in her throat.

"Gabriel." He steadied her with his hand.

"What?" she asked through the haze in her mind.

"I am Gabriel," he repeated. "Alexander is my twin."

Madeline stared at him. His eyes glimmered with humor, a smile permanently affixed to his lips.

"He did not tell you, did he?" Gabriel ran his hand over the scruff on his jaw. "We are identical twins."

Madeline stood in shock, her gaze bouncing back and forth between Gabriel and Evelyn. Her cousin approached her, wrapping her in a warm embrace.

"No harm done, Maddy," she whispered. "I am so glad you have returned." She released her and gestured toward Angus and Heather. "I see you have brought guests."

"Aye," Madeline said, shaking her head and remembering her etiquette. "This is my brother, Angus, and my sister, Heather."

Heather nodded, and then disappeared into the stables with the horses.

"Welcome home." Evelyn grinned, placing her hand in her husband's.

"So Alexander is not here?" Madeline asked, turning back to Evelyn and Gabriel. "We need to find him. Guards!"

"Maddy." Evelyn took her by the arm.

"We have not seen him." Gabriel's smile faded, his brow furrowed. "What has happened?"

"Come." Angus stepped forward. "We have much to tell you."

"We will find him," Gabriel said as Madeline twisted her skirt in her hands. "I promise."

Evelyn pulled her closer, embracing her. "It will be all right, love. Come inside, and we can discuss what to do next." Madeline followed them into the great hall.

As Angus relayed the events of the past week to Gabriel, Madeline found herself staring into the hearth where a small fire danced. If they caught him trying to escape, they would kill him.

"Here, drink this," Evelyn said, thrusting a goblet in her hands. "It will calm your nerves."

"Do I truly look so distraught?"

"Aye." Evelyn brushed a strand of hair from Madeline's face. "Gabriel will know what is to be done."

"I am glad you are safe," Madeline confessed, remembering the last time she saw her cousin. "Alexander told me you returned for the tournament, but then Angus snatched me away and in all the commotion..." She shrugged. "Are you happy?" Madeline glanced at Gabriel, seeing Alexander in every detail of his expression.

Angus and Gabriel were deep in conversation. They walked toward the door and entered the courtyard. Madeline turned her attention back to Evelyn.

"I love him. He is a good man, and he understands what my freedom means to me." Her cousin blushed, the red staining her cheeks. Evelyn lowered her voice to a whisper, "He is an incredible lover."

"You married him already?" Madeline's mouth dropped open when Evelyn nodded.

"What about you and Alexander?" Evelyn asked. "Has he finally told you how madly in love with you he is?"

"How did you..." She felt the heat rise in her cheeks.

"Before you disappeared, I confronted Alexander about his feelings for you." She grinned. "He denied them of course, but I am no fool. I could see the heated longing in his gaze when your back was turned."

Madeline felt as though her face burned in front of a fire. "He...well, we..." She stumbled over the words. "We were married just a few nights ago at his mother's home."

"Madeline Campbell!" Evelyn squealed as she wrapped her arms around her cousin. "Why...how...you must tell me everything."

They sat together in the great hall, and she told her of everything that had transpired over the time they had been gone. Evelyn stared at her, shock and elation written all over her face at the news of her marriage.

"Now we are truly sisters." Evelyn hugged her again.

"Maddy, come quick." Heather's voice broke into their conversation. The two women rushed to where Heather stood in the doorway leading out into the bailey.

"They better not be leaving without telling us," Evelyn said, pushing through the door, Madeline following close behind her.

Turning to Heather, she said, "You stay here. Find the cook, tell her I sent you, and keep out of trouble." Heather nodded and disappeared into the keep.

Madeline stormed into the courtyard where Angus and Gabriel stood with a half a dozen men, mounting their horses.

"I am coming with you," she said, motioning for the stable boy. "Saddle my horse, Nicholas, and be quick about it if you please."

"Aye, my lady," the young boy said as he nodded and disappeared into the stable.

"Madeline," Angus said with a resigned sigh as he turned to face her. "You cannot come with us."

"And why ever not? Alexander is my husband." She placed both hands on her hips.

"I am coming as well."

Madeline turned to see Evelyn standing next to her with arms crossed. She nodded at her cousin, and they stood side by side, staring at Angus as if daring him to defy both of them.

"There is no dissuading them, Angus," Gabriel said from

atop his horse. "I have seen that look far too many times to know they will only follow us once we leave these walls."

Angus sighed. "Och, woman, you had better listen. I will not have you performing heroics."

"Angus Campbell, did you just call me *woman*?" Madeline stood there, her mouth agape. "One day, you will say those words, and it will land you in a very uncomfortable position." Madeline snatched the reins from the stable boy and mounted her horse. With a glance behind her, she saw Evelyn astride her gelding, a grin on her lips.

"I knew I would be a good influence on you," Evelyn said, the pride evident in her tone. "Let us ride." Her cousin nudged her horse into a canter toward the main gate. Gabriel followed behind her, joined by the other knights in plain garb.

Madeline glanced at her brother again. He was shaking his head. She knew Angus would never understand her desire to go to her husband's aid. He had never been in love. He never knew the fear of losing something so precious, so pertinent to survival. Alexander needed her. She clicked to her mount, urging him forward.

They needed to get to Alexander before McLairn did something drastic and she was forced to make him pay for her suffering.

Alexander's hand cramped. He paused, resting the knife against the rope. Darkness had settled on the forest. He felt the rope give under his slow administration of the blade. *Soon.* It had not been long since McLairn had left him. The soft ebb and flow of a woman's sobs reached him. He glanced around the camp. A small fire flickered about a hundred feet in front of him. The men milled around it, barely conscious of anything around them. They had been drinking most of the day.

He began cutting the rope again. His mind fogged by the pain, Alexander found it hard to concentrate. *If only I had not gone back for Father's sword.* After a few moments of intense focus, the ropes loosened. Without bringing attention to himself, he gently slid the ropes from his wrists and hid his hands in his lap. A man stood by the fire and stumbled toward him. Alexander kept his breathing calm as the man came closer. He made an abrupt turn to the right and proceeded to piss, leaning against a large tree.

Alexander released the breath he had been holding when he heard the gentle song of a nightingale. He paused, focusing his attention on the sound. It came again, this time louder, closer. He chuckled, wincing from the action. Only one person alive could do such a terrible impersonation of a bird. *Gabriel.*

The man pissing just a few feet away dropped like a stone. The shadows materialized into a solid form. Something landed on Alexander's right shoulder. He turned to see a hooded figure leaning close to him, touching him.

"Are you well?" a familiar voice asked.

"Lady Evelyn?" Alexander spoke, his hoarse voice barely above a whisper.

"Aye," she whispered. "Can you walk?"

Alexander nodded, his gaze darting back to the men encamped around the fire.

"Do not worry, the men have them surrounded," she said as if reading his mind. "Come with me."

"But—" he hesitated "—I must save her."

"Who?"

"Madeline," he murmured, knowing the fate remaining for her if he did not stop McLairn.

"My cousin is safe," Evelyn said. "She is waiting with the horses."

Alexander shook his head. "I heard her screaming."

Evelyn reached up to feel his head. "You are feverish. Trust me, Alexander."

Gabriel appeared from the embrace of the shadows and knelt beside Evelyn. "Come."

He closed his eyes. "Gabriel, save her."

"Save who?" Gabriel asked, glancing at Evelyn. She shook her head. "Save who, Alexander?"

"I heard her scream," he said again.

"I will do what I can." Gabriel promised. "Get him out of here." The two of them pulled Alexander to his feet.

"Put your weight on me," Evelyn said, taking control. Gabriel slipped away into the darkness. Alexander leaned against her, following where she led.

As they approached the horses, a figure ran toward them. "Alexander."

He sighed as her voice wrapped around him. "Maddy, you are alive." He sighed, relief washing over him. She slid her arms around his waist and held him. Evelyn backed away, allowing them a moment.

"Of course I am," she said, kissing his stubbled cheek. "Why would I not be?"

"McLairn," he said, stroking her hair. "He had you. I heard you screaming."

"Och, the fever must have set in." Madeline reached up and pressed her cool hand to his head. She glanced at Evelyn.

One of the knights walked up. "Have you found a woman yet?"

"Nay, my lady. There is no lady among the brigands."

Alexander groaned and saw Madeline and Evelyn exchange worried expressions.

"We must get him to the keep. Quickly." Turning back to him, she smoothed his hair away from his face. He smiled at the tender gesture, weary.

"I love you," he whispered as the darkness rose and swirled around him, pulling him down.

Chapter Twenty-Five

Madeline hovered next to his bedside. Evelyn had assured her she had done right thing for his wound with the tools she had. Still, the fever raged. He had been asleep for four days. She sat in the chair next to his bed and dipped the rag into the cool water. Madeline hummed as she pressed the rag to his forehead. Evelyn used every potion and salve she knew to try to suppress the fever and kill the infection threatening to take him. While Madeline had confidence in her cousin's skills, at this point, she knew his fate lay in God's hands. Bowing her head, she whispered a prayer.

A knock at the door startled her. "Enter," she said, continuing to cool her husband's fevered brow.

Evelyn entered, followed by Heather. The girl rushed to Madeline's side, wrapping her arms around her older sister. Her eyes stayed on Alexander.

"Is he going to die?" she asked in a whisper. Her gaze flew to Evelyn and then Madeline. "He cannot die. He promised me..." Her voice broke as the words trailed off into quiet sobs.

"Och, hush now, lass," Madeline said, her brogue thickening as she gently stroked Heather's wild curls. "Come, let us take a walk in the garden." With a knowing look at Evelyn who nodded, she led her sister from the room and down the stairs. Once they stepped into the sunlight, Madeline caught a familiar scent coming from the kitchen.

"I know just what we need," Madeline said, pulling her sister toward the kitchen door. Slipping inside, they stood off to the side and watched as the cook kneaded dough. The maids bustled around them. She spotted the tray of fresh tarts and grabbed four of them. The duo retreated to the bailey again and made for the garden. Finding the old stone bench, they sat and ate in silence.

The garden was in full bloom and well maintained. Evelyn had been busy while she had been gone it seemed.

"Can I pick some flowers?" Heather asked, licking the fruit jam from her fingertips.

"Of course, be careful of thorns though." Madeline lingered as her sister bounded down the path, heading for a large patch of daisies and her namesake.

"She is quite a wild lass."

Madeline turned. Gabriel stood a few paces away. His dark blue doublet and black leggings made him appear quite dashing. Her heart ached. She forgot how much the brothers looked alike.

"Please sit," she said, gesturing to the bench beside her.

"Gra'mercy, my lady," he said as he sat. "So you are family now." His words were an observation, not a question. All the details of the happenings in Scotland over the past couple weeks were known to Gabriel, Evelyn, and the baron.

Madeline smiled at him, noting the levity in his blue eyes. He and Alexander might be twins, but the differences were obvious to her. She felt a blush rising at the sudden remembrance of her mistake a few days before. How could she have made such a blunder, kissing the wrong brother? Still mortified, she turned away, trying to hide her shame.

"That kiss is still bothering you, is it not?" He chuckled. "Do not worry overmuch, my dear sister, I promise never to tell Alexander."

"I must tell him," Madeline said, meeting his gaze again. "I keep no secrets from my husband."

"You two deserve each other," Gabriel said. "Duty and honor until the bitter end. Both of you."

"Was that meant to be a compliment, Sir Gabriel?" She cocked her head to the side, watching him closely.

"Aye." He cleared his throat. "He is fortunate to have you, my lady."

Her heart warmed at his words, yet it still ached with worry. "Do you think he will live?"

"I am hale and hearty, thanks to the healing knowledge of my lovely wife." He captured her hand in his and squeezed it. "'Twas barely a month ago, I had been in his place. Lying abed, a fever raging through me. I have every faith God will bring him through this, as he brought me."

"I thank you for your comforting words." She smiled at him.

He dropped her hands and stood. "I must go speak to the baron. May I visit my brother this evening?"

"You may visit him whenever you wish, good sir," she replied. He turned and left her in the sunlit gardens.

Heather ambled around the bend, a bouquet of flowers held against her chest. "Can we take these to Alexander?"

"Aye, my love."

They hurried back to the chamber where Alexander was recovering. Madeline pushed the door open and gasped. His blue eyes met hers.

"Maddy," Alexander said, his voice hoarse and weak.

Madeline rushed to his side. She sat on the bed, careful not to disturb him, and smoothed her hand over his hair.

"You are well," she said, her voice shaking with joy.

"Alexander!" Heather jumped up and down beside the bed. "I am so glad you are awake. Here, I brought these for you." She thrust the bouquet at him.

Evelyn accepted the flowers. "How about you and I go find some water to put these in?" She took Heather's hand and led her from the room.

Madeline returned her attention to her husband. "How are you feeling?"

"Weak," he said as he groaned. "I hate feeling weak. And helpless." He tried to sit up, but Madeline pushed him back down.

"You will stay in this bed until Evelyn says you are well enough to leave it," she said, her voice brooking no argument.

Alexander met her gaze, his eyes narrowing. He flinched, obviously still in pain. She tilted her head as if challenging him to test her resolve.

He harrumphed as he settled back against the pillows again. "What happened to McLairn and his men? Are they dead? Did they harm you?"

He would be fine. *Always duty first.* She shook her head.

"Not even awake five minutes, and this is what you ask me." She sighed. "They are in the dungeon being held until Angus returns. My brother will go home, gather some able men and return. McLairn and the remaining rebels will be escorted back to my father's estate for judgment." She squared her shoulders.

"Do you believe such a plan to be wise?" he asked. "They could escape."

"I believe my brother said something about a wagon, some very uncomfortable shackles, and a long walk to cool their heads." She grinned when Alexander nodded. "I do not know whether to blame your sour mood on your injury or these stone walls. It seems whenever you are here, you become so stiff and serious. I miss your smile."

"Madeline," he said hesitantly as if struggling to find the right words. "I may never be able to use this arm again. My days as a knight may be over. What will you do with a crippled husband?"

She smoothed a stray lock of hair away from his face. "The baron and Gabriel told me you would worry about that." She leaned close, taking his face between her hands. "I do not care whether you are a gilded lord, a penniless farmer, or a crippled knight. You are my husband, the man I love. I will stand by your side, come what may."

A small smile split his lips. "You truly are an angel," he whispered in reverence.

"You need to rest, take time and recover properly. No rushing it," she said, pressing a kiss to his lips. "Time will reveal what the next stage of our life shall be."

"As long as I have you by my side." He closed his eyes as she kissed him again, letting his lips linger against hers. When Madeline leaned back, she sighed. "What is wrong?" he asked.

"There is something you should know." She glanced at the door then back at him. "The night we escaped and reached the keep...I mistook your brother for you."

"We are identical twins." He smirked. "I can understand why."

She hesitated for a moment. "Aye, but you never told me

you had an identical twin." Madeline paused. "I did not know..." She trailed off waiting for the realization to hit him.

Alexander's eyes flew open wide. "You did not." He stared at her, his jaw gaping.

"I assumed he was you. I was so glad you had escaped. I did not care how you beat us to the keep. It all moved so quickly." She rambled on, finally meeting his gaze, the heat suffusing her face. "I kissed Gabriel."

Madeline waited for him to rage, yell, or worse, shun her. She licked her lips, a pit of worry burrowing into her gut as she waited for him to speak.

"Bloody hell, say something," she begged.

Alexander burst into laughter. His whole body shook with the power of it. It filled the room. A knock at the door startled her. Gabriel, Evelyn, and Heather stood in the doorway, their jaws hanging as if they had just witnessed a holy miracle.

"Is he...laughing?" Gabriel asked, his expression one of pure surprise. "What did you say to him?"

Madeline hid her face behind her hand as the laughter wrapped around her. She began to laugh at the absurdity of it all.

"You kissed my wife!" Alexander's words broke from between bouts of laughter. His eyes were wet with tears. He reached up and clutched his injured shoulder, wincing with pain.

"Now enough," Evelyn said, taking command of the situation. "You will tear the stitches, damn you." Gabriel and Heather joined in the laughter. "You two. Out. You can return once you have regained use of your senses."

Madeline stifled the giggles still welling up inside her. Alexander took a few deep breaths to steady himself and regain some composure. His eyes still glistened with laughter.

"I fail to see the humor in this," Madeline said, trying to hide behind her hand.

Evelyn peeled back the bandage to check the wound. She worked efficiently, not saying a word, but Madeline noticed a smile playing at the corners of her cousin's lips.

"Och," he said on a sigh. "*Mo chridhe.*"

Madeline slid her hand in his, smoothing her fingers over

his callused palm. "Do you forgive me?"

"There is naught to forgive. 'Twas partly my fault for not telling you of my twin, and his charming good looks." He grinned, and she melted at the sight.

"Aye," Evelyn said.

Alexander and Madeline glanced at her in unison. Evelyn glanced up from the wound. "Oh, well, um...I shall just leave you two alone again. Wound is healing properly." She turned and left the room in haste, a rose blush high on her cheeks.

"She means well," Madeline said.

"I know." Alexander wound his hand around the back of her neck and pulled her down. She leaned against his body, kissing him again.

"I love you," she whispered against his mouth.

"I know that too," he said. "I have known it for a while now."

She pushed at him, but his grip tightened, holding her close. "Are you always going to be so certain of yourself?"

"Aye."

"Good. Now, you need to rest," she said, untangling his fingers from her hair.

Alexander frowned, his brow furrowed. "Are you always going to be so demanding?"

"Aye."

He grinned.

Madeline settled into the chair beside the bed and picked up her needlework. "Tell me about when you were a wee lad," she said.

Alexander began with a story of his father teaching him, Gabriel, and James how to shoot a bow. The stories continued, and a bond began to forge between them. They fell into comfortable conversation as the day faded into night, and the shadows were brought to light.

Chapter Twenty-Five

Several Months Later

The full moon illuminated the road. Alexander glanced over his shoulder, his hands tightening on the reins as he shifted his weight in the saddle. He heard Gabriel snicker.

"They are not following us," Gabriel said finally voicing Alexander's worst fear.

"I pray you are right." Alexander met his brother's gaze. "Both of them need to stay behind those walls. They are..."

"Expecting." Gabriel finished his sentence. "You are just terrified to be a father, are you not?"

"Not terrified." He cleared his throat. He remembered the indescribable joy and fear he had felt when Madeline told him she was expecting their first child. "Just a bit apprehensive is all. You are certain they stayed in the keep. I know how those two get restless."

"There is naught to concern yourself with. 'Tis the middle of the night. When they wake in the morning, Angus and the baron will be sure to keep them occupied."

Alexander glanced at his brother. It amazed him how Gabriel fell into the role of husband and knight. Both of them had given up the hood, but danger still lurked on the border. Tension between the English and Scottish had increased since Robert the Bruce's death. The reivers were bolder than ever, and Alexander became increasingly aware of mounting tensions with France. His country was slowly being pulled in different directions. They needed to speak with James about finding some new recruits for the role of Shadow Guardian to ensure the safety of those living on the border.

"What do you think of Angus?" Alexander asked.

"You know I like him. He is a good strong lad with a

proficient sword hand. Why do you ask?"

"I think he would make a good Shadow Guardian, would he not?"

Gabriel ran his hand through his hair carelessly. "Of course, if he has a mind for it. Does he have a lass waiting for him somewhere?"

"Nay, not that I am aware." Alexander shook his head. "The one time I ever saw him lose his wits for a lass was at the inn on our journey south a few months ago. She had him so twisted up, then knocked him out with some kind of herbal concoction and stole his coin. I have never seen him so mortified. I think it has made him swear off women."

Gabriel laughed. "Little wonder he keeps to himself when the barmaids try to catch his attention."

"What say you? Shall we make him our brother in Shadow as well?"

"Aye." Gabriel wiped a tear from his eye. "Angus would make a good ally and a consistent leader. We need someone on the Scottish side, and I do not think he would guide us astray."

"I shall send a letter to James when we return, informing him of our decision. We may need to recruit another man or two."

Gabriel waved his hand. "One battle at a time, Alexander. You have not lost your touch, I will grant you that."

"What of our mother and sisters?" Alexander could not help but address the question burning in the back of both of their minds.

"Mother will not be swayed to leave her homestead, not unless we give her a reason to do so." Gabriel chuckled. "I think it is about time we informed her of the new role she is about to fill."

"Aye," Alexander said, nodding. "Once we tell her both our wives are expecting, I believe she may want to be closer to be with the bairns. You are clever."

"I do have moments of pure genius," Gabriel bragged. "What the baron will do with a house full of women, I know not."

"He did grant us both our own estates. Perhaps we should move onto the next chapter of our lives?" Alexander thought about the baron's wedding present to his daughter and niece. The estates were small, but fertile farms positioned just outside the village, side by side. Truly they had been blessed with such a gracious gift.

"'Tis a wonder how things work out, is it not?"

"Aye." Alexander sucked in a sharp breath as he rolled his shoulder gently. It ached and stiffened with repetitive motion, especially on stormy days. Evelyn had worked with him to regain the use of his arm. She held vast knowledge when it came to herbs and healing.

Madeline had also taken an interest in the art since his injury. Having two wise women in one barony had become a blessing for everyone. His chest swelled knowing his wife helped people, becoming the leader he knew she could be. Together they discovered the hidden talents they both possessed and nurtured them.

He sighed, longing for her touch. The wind picked up, and he pulled his cloak close, shielding him from the chill of its bite. "How is your side?"

"Better," Gabriel replied. "The cold makes it ache something fierce though." He pulled his cloak tighter as well.

"The sooner we finish this, the quicker we can return to our beds...and our wives." Alexander grinned.

"Aye, you do not have to tell me twice." Gabriel nodded. "Let us find Richard and end this tonight."

"With pleasure." Alexander pulled his hood up and nudged his horse into a trot, with Gabriel following close behind.

About the Author

Kirsten S. Blacketer is a multi-published indie author of both historical and contemporary romance. When she's not writing, she homeschools her two children and enjoys time with her family. In those moments of freedom, she devours romance novels while sipping a glass of wine. Age has only shown her that writing villains can be just as fun as heroes. Her next life goals are to write a New York Times Bestseller and one day have Adam Driver play a starring role in a film version of one of her books. A girl can dream, right?

Read more at **http://kirstensblacketer.com.**

ALSO WRITES AS JEN BRADLEE

Other Books by Kirsten S. Blacketer

Craving 1985 Series
When I Found You
Can't Fight This Feeling
She Gives Love a Bad Name
Owner of a Lonely Heart
Just What I Needed

Historical
An Irresistible Shadow
A Shadow's Kiss
Mississippi Moonshine
Deceiving the Earl
Jewel of Winter
At Winter's Demand
Under Winter's Control
Seducing Winter's Gentleman
Stealing the Widow's Heart
Seduction on the Alpine Express
Temptation on the Alpine Express

Contemporary
A Lockdown Love Affair
A Holiday Love Affair
Mistletoe and Mistakes
Confessions of a Fangirl
Confessions of a Gamer Girl
Confessions of a Glamour Girl

Fantasy/FairyTale
Curse of the Huntsman's Jewel
The Huntsman's Revenge

Pirates and Persuasion
Queen Takes Hook